All That We Are Book One

BY ELICIA ROPER

Cover design by Natalia Ava
Editing by Caron Pescatore
PAPERBACK ISBN: 9798780116677

Trigger Warnings:
Death, illness and abandonment.

Age Rating:
12 and up

Dedication:

THIS BOOK IS DEDICATED to anyone who has ever felt that they are not good enough. I want you to know that you *are* enough. A thousand times enough, and you will find someone who will love you, all of you, for all that you are.

-E.R.

Playlist:

"Minefields"-Faouzia, John Legend
"Dream"- Shawn Mendes
"The Few Things"- JP Saxe
"It's You"- ZAYN
"Used To This"- Camila Cabello
"Anyway"- Noah Kahan
"If You Want Love"- NF
"Angel"- The Weeknd
"Exit Wounds"- The Script
"Half A Man"- Dean Lewis
"Falling"- Harry Styles
"There You Are"- ZAYN
"Losing Me"- Gabrielle Aplin, JP Cooper
"Standing With You"- Guy Sebastian
"Easy"- Camila Cabello
"Fix Me Up"-Fin Argus, Sabrina Carpenter
"Fix You"- Coldplay
"I Feel Your Pain" - Famba, David Aubrey
To listen on Spotify, CLICK HERE[1].

Prologue:

BATTLE FACE ON, ATHENA pulls her hair into a ponytail, carefully selecting her weapon of destruction. Crowbar in hand, she pulverizes her unsuspecting victim. Violet steps in tow beside her as she grasps a firm grip on the baseball bat, taking a swing.

The glass pops as it shatters, exploding like fireworks throughout the dimly lit room. The thunderous bass of the music pulsated through their veins like bursts of epinephrine.

It's invigorating-she feels vibrant and alive as she continues to mercilessly destroy everything in sight. From TVs to Printers, everything is smashed to smithereens, wires and cords dangling lifelessly.

Athena takes a deep breath, completely satisfied.

She welcomes a release from the troublesome thoughts weighing on her mind. She smiles at her partner in crime, Violet, who smiles back valiantly.

Violet is her ride-or-die. Through thick and thin, she is always by her side. The two have been inseparable ever since they met in kindergarten.

Proud of their work, Violet puts an arm around Athena's shoulder. "All that angst and anger worked up my appetite. I'm starving; let's go eat."

"Yes, ma'am." She salutes her like a soldier getting ready for battle.

The two zip down their white hazmat suits and return their safety gear to the front desk. "Wreck-It-Ralph" is the ultimate stress reliever, where you can wipe away all your pain and anxieties in a single blow. For about six years now, this has become a go-to place for when they need to take the edge off.

She stepped outside and let the fresh air fill her lungs, feeling refreshed and calm. High sunlit clouds drifted across a clear blue sky. Lifting her face skyward, she closes her eyes.

Ah, this is nice.

CHAPTER 1
Athena:

SOME LIKE A BRIGHT and sunny day, the streets bustling with laughter and excitement. Yet, I find that comfort and solace lie in the tranquil sound of the rain. The world outside is at a standstill, eerily peaceful and quiet. The cold streak from the rain blows in, so I wrap my blanket tighter around my shoulders. The hot steam from the mug warms my face as I take a sip from it.

The words are forever ingrained in my mind, but each time I read them, it still feels so fresh and raw, like an open wound that has not had enough time to heal. Putting the letters away, I pack them neatly, closing the ivory felt box and storing it back in its place—the dresser drawer beside the white canopy bed.

My phone buzzes on the nightstand. I smile when I see a text from my best friend Violet, also known as V. Violet, who has always been spontaneous. The type to randomly plan trips and excursions and make spur-of-the-moment decisions.

Violet: Girl, clear your calendar for tomorrow. We are going to Wonderland! The first one to throw up buys the funnel cakes.

Athena: Challenge accepted. I'll bring the barf bag, but don't be fooled; I'm bringing it for you.

Violet: Oh, you've got jokes. It's on.

Violet tells me to make sure that I do not dress like a homeless person. Clearly, she has every intention of setting me up. I can already picture the cheeky look on Violet's face, but that doesn't mean I'm caving in to her latest attempt at matchmaking.

Athena: I'm just going to pretend you didn't say that.

The following day, the sun slices through my window, casting a warm glow throughout the room. Jumping out of bed, I head to my closet to decide what to wear to Wonderland today.

Opening the grey metal doors of the closet, I scan my wardrobe, debating for a bit. I will put a little effort into what I wear today. Not because Violet asked me to, but because *I* want to. I slip into a boat-neck mustard-yellow tee that goes great with my rich hazelnut complexion and tuck the tee into a brand-new pair of dark blue high-waisted jeans. Pulling my hair out of a ponytail, I let the chocolate brown curls cascade over my shoulders.

I bound down the stairs and pranced toward the closet by the front door to grab a pair of sneakers.

I say goodbye to mom, who is watching TV, and head outside just as Violet's black Audi pulls up the driveway. Violet is smiling from ear to ear. Clear evidence that something is up.

Seeing right through her façade, I give Violet my most menacing stare. "What are you up to?" I ask, hopping inside and buckling the seat belt.

"Nothing! Nothing at all." Violet insists, her voice a few octaves higher than normal—a telltale sign that she is lying.

Violet's blue eyes glisten, and she gives me a teasing smile. I can't help but crack a tiny smile as she turns on the radio, cranking it up to full volume. We belt out the words to every song, dancing along like nobody's watching.

Except they *are*. A curly-haired lady in a red convertible gives us a questioning look as she passes by. She probably thinks we look like fools, but who cares?

. . ⌀ . .

The parking lot is abuzz with people shuffling in and out. We arrive at the front entrance and waltz over to stand in line. Violet keeps glancing over my shoulder as if she's looking for someone.

"V, you did not." I turn to face her.

"What?" Violet asks all innocently.

"I thought it was supposed to be just us!" Although 11 years of friendship have taught me that Violet would be the type to surprise me with something like this, since she keeps trying to break me out of my shell, I hoped she didn't.

"Relax," Violet says, reading my thoughts. "Don't worry your pretty little head about it. It'll be just fine."

I'm not so convinced.

"You just might have some fun," Violet sings.

Feeling my resolve slipping away, I give up the fight.

That's when I see him—standing a little farther off from the rest of them, his chest shaking with laughter.

Snap out of it.

I tell myself to stop staring like a creep before he catches me, or worse, before Violet sees. She would never let me live it down. Looking away, I peer over in V's direction, but it is far too late. Violet is staring back with a sly smirk on her face.

Busted.

"Don't you dare," I warn, knowing full well Violet will immediately overreact and start planning our wedding the second she gets it into her head I might be interested in him.

Violet backs away, putting her hands up in surrender. "My lips are sealed."

After waiting in the long line, Violet & I link arms, skipping toward the lines for the rollercoaster rides. The rest of the people Violet invited to tag along to join us.

"Hello, thank you all for joining." Violet turns her attention to all of us. "This beautiful brunette here is my best friend, Athena. And yes, lucky for you, she is also single."

Violet grins at me. Wishing the ground would just open and swallow me, I try to laugh off the embarrassment.

"Hello, please disregard everything my friend says. As you all probably already know, she is a little crazy," I say awkwardly.

"Whatever." Violet rolls her eyes but still chuckles at the implication. "Athena, meet Vanessa, Melody, Jake, Damon, and Caiden."

Violet, Melody, Vanessa, and I run up to grab front row seats, and after squeezing in, pull the padded arm down over our heads. Melody pulls out her camera to record the ride.

I absolutely love rollercoasters. I go for the thrill: it is simply exhilarating! My stomach fills with butterflies as I brace myself for the steep 80-degree drop. Then, the ride takes off with rushing intensity, and my stomach drops with every sharp turn. Every twist sends my head spinning. The rushing adrenaline feels near to bursting out of my veins.

This high is the best part of roller coaster rides.

Caiden:

ATHENA IS ABSOLUTELY stunning.

When she smiles, there is this glow about her. Looking for a chance to talk to her, I stick around when the others leave to grab lunch.

"That's okay, you guys. Go ahead; I'll meet you back here." Athena shoos them off. Going ahead to the Leviathan line, she smiles that radiant smile of hers to tell them she will be fine.

I offer to stick around with her. She shrugs. "Okay, if it's okay with you, it's fine by me." Athena glances at me for a moment, then asks, "So how do you know V?"

"We were in the same pottery class."

"Oh cool, I've never tried pottery before. What's it like?" She asks curiously.

"Brilliant. Astonishingly, we can create beautiful, sculptural, and functional pieces with our own hands." I assume I must have a look on my face as I described it because a slow smile spreads across her face.

"Wow, that sounds fantastic."

With a wide grin, I invite her to join me. "I'll have to show you sometime."

Athena opens her mouth to reply and then closes it shut when her stomach grumbles. She laughs in an attempt to cover it up.

"I'm starved! I'm going to grab some food. Do you want anything?" I offer, so she'll feel less embarrassed.

"Um, sure. I'll have whatever you're having."

Athena opens her bag to get her wallet; I wave it off. "Don't sweat it. I'll be right back."

. . ༄ . .

Running off to buy food, I rack my brain, trying to figure out what she would like to eat. There are rows and rows of food carts, ranging from burgers, sushi, Thai, pizza, and New York Fries. Sushi and Thai would have been okay if that is your taste, but just in case, let's pick something safe. Everyone loves pizza. Perfect. Settling on pizza, I go ahead to order.

Walking over to her, I take note of a guy in a striped shirt talking to her. He is clearly flirting with her, and Athena looks like she wants to bite off his head.

Putting an arm around her shoulder, flashing him a smile, I ask, "Is this jerk bothering you?"

"Not anymore. He was just leaving." Athena narrows her eyes.

The guy mutters something under his breath and walks away.

The minute he leaves, I move my arm. "Sorry. I-"

She smiles. "Don't sweat it. I'm glad you came. That guy refused to take no for an answer. Super irritating."

"I wonder if I saved you or him because you looked like you were ready to kill the guy."

"Well, I guess we will never know," Athena says with a smirk.

The rest of the gang swarm in, and we all hover around the table to eat lunch, exchange phone numbers, and say our goodbyes.

. . ༄ . .

Back at home, as soon as I walk through the front door, Luna's sitting on her favorite yellow couch by the window. She is wagging her tail with her tongue hanging out, happy to see me. "Come here, girl." I pat my legs to get her to come over. Luna pounces on me, tackling me to the floor. "I missed you too." Laughing, she licks my face.

With a smile, I walk into the kitchen where Mom is cooking. Coming up behind her, I wrap my arms around her, planting a kiss on her cheek.

"You look like you're in a good mood," Ashley says as she cuts up the green onions. "Did you have fun with your friends today?"

"Yeah, it was great."

It looks like Mom is making one of my favorites- "Firecracker Chicken." This recipe consists of crispy breaded chicken tossed in a sweet and spicy sauce served over a bed of rice. Mom usually pairs it with "Spinach and Feta Cheese Borek," which has delicious layers of phyllo sheets smothered in spinach and feta cheese.

For dessert, I will make my little sister Isabella's favorite dish—"Tulumba." It's a special type of dough that's deep-fried and soaked in sweet syrup. Crunchy on the outside, soft and juicy on the inside.

I roll up my sleeves so I can wash my hands and help.

Drawn in by the sweet aroma of the food, Isabella comes bouncing down the hardwood stairs. Mom tells her to stop running down the stairs, or she will slip and fall.

"No, I won't," Isabella says confidently. "I'm not clumsy like Caiden. Unlike him, I know how to keep my balance."

I playfully hit her behind the head with the oven mitt.

"Hey!" Isabella rubs the back of her head.

CHAPTER 2
Caiden:

THE POTENT SCENT OF motor oil and gasoline lingers in the air, but I'm no longer fazed by it. After working here for almost five years, I have become immune to the smell.

Taking a walk around the shop, I quietly observe to see what the others are working on. They are hard at work right now, fixing up old vehicles and resurrecting them back to life so that they are as good as new. There is something so gratifying and satisfying about working with your hands and accomplishing a task.

The day has gone by surprisingly fast. Looking down at my watch, I can see it is already 2 o'clock. We have worked through lunchtime. "It's time for a break," I call out to everyone.

"Finally!" Jake hangs his head back with an exhausted expression on his face. Jake didn't get in until 10 a.m., so he hasn't even worked as long as the rest of us. He tends to be a tad bit melodramatic at times.

"Oh, please don't be so dramatic. You barely even lifted a finger all this time." Drew wrings his wet towel, slapping Jake on the back of his neck. Drew, Jake, and I started working at the "Mint Auto Repair" together, so we have gotten pretty used to each other. Granted, Jake gets picked on the most, but we do it with love.

"Where should we go out for lunch? I'm craving BBQ," Damon says, scrolling through his phone for places to eat. Damon always comes up with the best places to eat, so of course, we trust his decision. "Let's head to Daryll's Steakhouse," he suggests.

Everyone nods in agreement and shuffles out of the garage.

"Hey man, are you coming?" Drew stays back to ask me before walking out with the others.

"Yeah, I'm just going to finish up here first," I tell him.

Drew gives me his all-time favourite, 'Are you for real' look.

Okay, to be fair, I do tend to drag my feet sometimes, but that's only because I like to complete a task once I've started working on it. I'm not a fan of stopping right in the middle of a task. I doubt that I have all that much to do. The car I'm working on looks like it just needs a few finishing touches, and then it will be all done.

Laughing, I promise I'll catch up with them. "It'll be quick, promise. I'll meet you guys there."

As soon as I pop open the hood of the car, thick black smoke comes pouring out. Shielding my face with my arm, I try to break up the smoke. I have my work laid out for me with this one, but it will be more than worth it. A 1960s Jaguar—she is a beauty. Not only does this car have an impeccably styled auto body, but it is also extremely comfortable. The Jaguar brand is all about style and speed; it is truly a high-performance vehicle at its best, a luxury brand that is well worth every penny invested.

Reaching into the toolbox on the floor, I sift through the pile of tools for the pliers. After working on the car for a bit, my left hand starts to cramp. Flexing my fingers, I try to alleviate the tension and get the blood flowing again. Right now, my hands feel like they are being stabbed with pins and needles. It's only momentary discomfort, though; it will pass. It always does.

In the quietness of the room, I'm all alone with nothing but my thoughts.

There is not a day that goes by that I do not think of *him*.

My phone rings, snapping me out of the trance—

"Bro, are you coming?" I can practically hear the agitation in Jake's voice over the phone for having them waiting so long.

"Sorry, man, I'll be right out," I say, hoping he is not too mad. Thankful for the distraction, I head outside.

. . ❧ . .

After lunch, the guys head back to the shop to finish up what they were working on. Xavier, the owner of the Jaguar, is already on his way. Wiping the beads of sweat covering my forehead, I get straight to work. After a few hours, the car engine starts up, and it looks all ready to go.

A man with dark sunglasses dressed in a black suit walks up to the garage door.

Xavier is here.

I throw the keys to Jake so he can take Xavier with him for a test drive. "Here are the keys. Go take it out for a spin."

"Who, me? Why don't *you* take it for the test drive since you're the one that fixed it?" Jake asks before Damon pulls him aside, pushing him out the door.

"But there's just one thing I don't get, though," Jake says, scratching his head.

Damon laughs at him, with Shawn and the others joining in. "Only one?"

"Ha-ha, funny." Jake laughs it off, not caring that he is being teased, but then his face is more serious when he asks Drew, "Why is it he works at a mechanic shop and fixes cars but doesn't drive one?"

"What do you mean?" Shawn asks, confused. Shawn has not worked at the shop as long as the others and hasn't had an opportunity to notice that I don't drive any of the cars that we work on.

Drew shuts Jake up, clamping a hand over his mouth. "Don't mind him. He... he doesn't know what he's talking about."

CHAPTER 3

Athena:

"OKAY, BEFORE WE GO in, let's go over some ground rules." Violet narrows her eyes at me. "So, what are we going to do?"

"Stop scowling, or you'll get a permanent frown on your face," I say with a teasing smile.

Violet squeezes her eyes shut in response and pinches the bridge of her nose. "Don't make me put a leash on you."

"Alright, alright. Somebody's a bit testy this morning. Clearly, you haven't had your morning coffee." I smile for good measure before adding, "Look, but don't touch. I got it."

"Good. Good. Glad we are on the same page here."

"C'mon, guys, let's go!" Sky yells to us from the other side of the water fountain. My sister can be so bossy at times.

We stroll through the mall, Sky tugging on my arm, dragging me into all the stores she wants to go to, which leads us to an arts and crafts store similar to Michael's. Sky insists that we go in to look for the art set that her friend Isabella is crazy about.

Running my hand along the multicoloured fabrics, I am fascinated by the wide array of colors. I have always admired anyone that can bring out the beauty of art, mostly because it's not my area of expertise.

It takes me no more than a millisecond to spot the bookstore behind the store. The shiny new books are sparkly and gleaming. I long for them as I stare through the store's glass window. When no one's looking, I sneak off, my eyes on the prize.

Violet & Sky:

VIOLET FRANTICALLY looks around the store, seeing no sign of Athena. "Where is she?"

"How am I supposed to know?" Sky says.

Violet peers over Sky's shoulders and notices the bookstore next door. She starts marching out of the store, motioning for Sky to help look for Athena.

"Why should I?" Sky groans in protest, not seeing how or why she should care enough to help look for Athena.

"Maybe because you weren't watching her like you were supposed to?" Violet says.

"Excuse me, last time I checked, I wasn't my sister's keeper. She is *your* responsibility. Not mine."

Athena:

I'M CRADLING BOOKS upon books in my arms, along with a shopping cart I filled to the brim with even *more* books.

Okay, so I might have a teensy-weensy problem. I wouldn't go so far as to say I'm a book hoarder... but I do *love* books.

Unfortunately, it does not take Violet long to find me. "Drop it," Violet says, stepping toward me. I pretend not to hear her and instead start rapidly putting the books on the counter, waiting for the cashier to scan them.

Violet does not step down, though. "Step away from the cart." It is now a power play as the two of us lock eyes in a staring competition.

The first one to blink or look away loses.

The cashier attempts to speak to us, but she is ignored since neither of us is ready to back down. This charade earns some intense stares as people scoot around us to stand in line. I'm the first one to give up.

Man, I always lose in staring competitions.

I follow Violet out of the store, my lips pressed together, unimpressed, without uttering another word.

We continue walking around the mall for a little more, our next stop, Bubble Tea. Bubble Tea comes in so many varieties. There is something for everyone here. Whether you like fruit, black tea, or a sweet treat, there are a plethora of options to choose from. We collect our drinks from the counter and take a seat. Sky chose the Winter Melon Infusion; Violet and I both got the Coffee Supreme.

.. ⸙ ..

When I come back from the washroom, at the corner of my eye, I could have sworn I saw the flash of someone half-speed walking, half-sprinting just across from us on the opposite side of the Bubble Tea Shop. That's when I notice someone's missing. Violet's seat is now empty, although I could've sworn she was sitting right across from me 5 minutes earlier.

"Where is V?" I turn to Sky, who shrugs, staring at her phone, obviously having no idea Violet even left.

I shake my head, knowing full well *exactly* where Violet would go without telling me. "Come on, Sky, let's go."

'Play Pen,' you could say, was Violet's guilty pleasure. She knew better than to go into that store because whenever she did, it never ended well. It only made her wish for something she could never have—a pet.

I push open the wooden doors to the store, scanning for any signs of my blonde friend. Aha found her. Violet is happily playing peekaboo with a bunny rabbit.

"Nuh-uh." I shake my head.

Violet's lower lip starts to tremble. "But..."

"No buts."

"But look at that face!" Violet pleads, trying to persuade me. "How can you say *no* to that face?"

"I can't." By now, I have placed a hand over my eyes. It's the only way because otherwise, we would end up bringing home *all* the animals in here, then we would have to find *another* home to live in, for pulling a stunt like that. Needless to say, we have a no-pet rule at our house. "That's why I'm refusing to look."

"But A..." Violet whimpers.

"But nothing. You know better than me that your Mom would have your head served on a silver platter if you ever brought a pet home."

Violet does not budge, so I wrap my arm around her shoulders as I lead her out of the pet store. "I know, sweetie, I know," I soothe, knowing how much it hurts to have to say no.

· · ᢙᢙ · ·

That evening, the moon lit up the sky like a night light beaming a luminous glow. Upon hearing a knock on the door, I wonder, in surprise, who it could be since I wasn't expecting anyone tonight.

Our neighbor, Evan, is standing outside of the front door. "I'm so sorry to bother you with this so last minute. My wife's working late, and you guys were the only ones I could think of to ask," he rambles.

Evan and April have been tremendously kind neighbors for the past 15 years. They have become like family. Evan is the kind of person you could say wore his heart on his sleeve. He was never one to hide how he feels—it shows on his face.

I can tell that we really were his last resort, which is okay with me because I love kids, and Starr is simply adorable.

Evan furrows his brow in a mix of anxiety and frustration as he tells me that his mom, Iris, is getting discharged from the hospital today. He doesn't think it would be a good idea to bring Starr along. With her having such a weak immune system, it would be too much of a risk.

Starr tugs on his hand, trying to get her dad's attention, but he's too distracted to notice.

He must have a lot on his plate.

"No, no, that's perfectly okay. I adore Starr, and I would love to watch her." Starr is wide-eyed as she observes the conversation between us. "I'm glad Iris is doing better; that's fantastic news. Say hi to her for me, please," I say, hoping to reassure him we will be fine.

"Right, Starr? We're going to watch movies, eat popcorn, and have a great time." I lean down, smiling at her.

"Daddy, you're leaving me?" Starr asks in disbelief.

Evan crouches down on one knee to meet Starr at eye level. "Yes, sweetie, but Daddy's coming right back, okay?"

Starr shakes her head as she starts to cry. "No! No! Don't leave me!" she says frantically.

"Baby, I'll be right back. I promise." Evan assures her with a kiss on the cheek.

Evan blows her kisses as he walks out the door.

Starr latches onto his leg as she breaks out in sobs. "Please don't leave me," she pleads, tears streaming down her face.

There's a sinking feeling in my stomach as I watch Starr cling to her father's leg. I find myself fighting the lump forming in my throat. My voice is dry and chalky as I try to speak, but no words come out.

I need to breathe.

I squeeze my eyes shut to shake off the horrid memory I would love nothing more than to forget.

． ． ᄿᢅᢓᡐ ． ．

I awaken to the sound of someone frantically rummaging through drawers. I blink away the sleep from my eyes to follow the sound. Pulling the blanket around my bare shoulders, I cradle the teddy bear in my arms.

I walk ever so slowly down the hall, taking small quiet steps to not wake anyone. The door creaks as it opens. In the shadows of the darkness, Dad's there amidst the mess and clutter surrounding the floor. He hurriedly throws more clothes into the suitcase.

For a moment, he glances up at me, revealing the tears welling up in his eyes. Looking away, he wipes the tears from his eyes.

I pretend not to see it.

"Daddy?" I call out in a nervous quiver.

Dad doesn't respond.

He continues packing and closes the suitcase. When Dad gets up to leave the room, I latch onto his leg. "Daddy," I cry in between sobs.

"Why are you leaving me? What about Alex? And Mom? Don't you... don't you love us anymore?"

My teddy bear falls to the floor.

I squeeze his leg even tighter now, willing him not to let me go, to let *us* go.

. . ⚬ . .

"Athena? Are you okay?" Evan touches my arm.

I blink; my focus is blurry. All I can see is the hazy image in front of me of my dad's car driving away. "Yeah... yeah, I'm fine," I tell Evan, forcing a smile.

Starr grabs my hand.

CHAPTER 4
Athena:

A REGULAR DAY ENSUES with Mom yelling at Sky to hurry up and get ready for school. "Sky, let's go! You are going to be late for school. The bus comes in five minutes," Mom yells from the kitchen.

Of course, this is no surprise because Sky tends to wait until the very last second to get ready.

My younger brother Alex chomps down on his cereal, talking in between bites. "It wouldn't be the first or the *last* time, that's for sure."

Sky crossed her arms, unimpressed. "Shut up; this coming from the one who didn't even bother to show *up* to school?"

"Well, I eventually graduated, didn't I?"

Wow, how very noble of you. Congrats.

"Key word-*eventually*," Sky says.

Yep, hit the nail right on the head with that one. I give Sky a high five for that witty comeback.

"Ignore Alex. Let's go." Mom proceeds to push Sky out the door.

• • ໑ๆ໐ • •

Later, at home, Sky is giving Mom her oh-so-famous puppy dog eyes. Sky uses it to her advantage, that's for sure. If anyone else tried to pull it off, it would not have the same effect.

I poke Sky in the arm. "What is it you want this time?"

With a sly smirk on her face, Sky leaves me guessing. "Wouldn't *you* like to know?" she says and runs upstairs.

No more than five minutes later, Sky prances downstairs with a huge smile plastered on her face. Whatever plan she was concocting, she clearly got what she wanted.

Mom walks back downstairs, announcing that we have plans tonight. "Hurry up and get dressed. We are invited to go out tonight."

"Going where?" Rain inquires, looking up from her phone. My younger sister Rain is the quietest member of the family, but don't let that fool you. She can be pretty scary when she wants to be.

"Don't worry about it. Time is running out. We are leaving in less than 30 minutes. Tell your father to go start up the car."

Rain heads downstairs to the basement where Collin is working from home to relay Mom's message.

Back upstairs, Rain asks us if we know where we are going tonight. She is met with silence as we all ignore her, distracted by our phones.

"Why does no one ever tell me anything?" Rain says out loud to whoever is listening.

"Maybe because nobody likes you, that's why." Alex, being Alex, replies. You can always count on Alex to tell you how he really feels. He has no shame in telling you exactly what is on his mind.

• • ⁓ • •

After driving around for about twenty minutes, we arrive at our destination. The lawn is beautifully decorated with an array of flowers, and the house has a warm and cozy feel. Potted plants lie on the steps of the mint green and soft cream patio stones.

"Nicola! So nice to finally meet you and the family! Please come on in." A very pretty lady with blue eyes greets us with a bright smile.

The lady's name is Ashley, and she is Isabella's Mom. Isabella and Sky are friends from school. It turns out Isabella called and begged Mom to have her over, and Ashley thought it would be a great idea to invite all of us, too. Sky is really something. She knows just how to get what she wants; it is admirable, actually.

I'm also surprised that Caiden is Isabella's older brother. Who would have thought?

"Hope you guys like games!" Ashley says excitedly while whipping out the game of Monopoly.

Oh no. This is a disaster in the making.

"I'm sorry," I blurt out, feeling instantly embarrassed by what is about to take place.

"For what?" Caiden asks.

I shake my head solemnly. "For what you are about to see."

"Why are *you* talking? You don't even play," Alex spits back.

"Well, at least I don't manipulate."

Alex sits back with his arms crossed over his chest. "Hey man, don't hate the player; hate the game."

· · ◦❦◦ · ·

The game ensues, and as per usual, it gets ugly.

"Collin! Get out." Mom is clearly not pleased. "I can't play with you."

"Why? I didn't even do anything," Collin says.

Alex mutters under his breath, not buying it. "Oh, please stop pretending to be all innocent."

Collin throws his head back as he bursts into a deep-bellied laugh. The sound ripples into waves of laughter—like an infectious disease, it's contagious, as we join in too.

"You know exactly what you are doing. Stop trying to do some reverse psychology nonsense on me. It may work on the kids, but don't you dare try that foolishness with me." Mom crosses her arms over her chest.

"No, Daddy wouldn't trick us like that. Right, Daddy?" Sky gives Collin her puppy dog eyes.

Collin shakes his head. "Of course not, sweetie."

"Oh! So, we're outright lying now?" Rain says.

"Okay, I'm just going to take my $200 for passing go," I say, not wanting to be a part of this.

The embarrassment continues as it becomes evident that Collin is winning. Then the horror of all horrors happens when Mom lands on Collin's property.

The tension in the room is so thick you can cut it with a knife. All of Mom's properties have been mortgaged, with only a couple hundred dollars left to her name.

"That'll be $150," Collin points out, clearly oblivious to the impending situation.

Everyone except for Collin knows better than to mess with Mom.

"It was nice knowing you, Daddy." Sky pats him on the shoulder.

A look of disgust and utter disdain washes over Mom's face. She is livid. Collin nervously shifts his eyes to look anywhere else.

We hold our breath, waiting for what we know will happen next.

A loud beeping sound breaks the silence. "I'll go get that." Caiden gets up from his seat on the floor. He's probably relieved to get to run away from this madness, and I don't blame him at all.

If I could, I'd run too.

"Saved by the bell." I breathe a sigh of relief. It is way too early for the Alshaaers to see this side of our family.

"Cookies!" Isabella exclaims happily.

Caiden hands each of us a plate, and when he walks over to give me mine, I thank him.

"You're welcome," Caiden replies with a smile as we lock eyes. Alex clears his throat, so we look away.

In between bites, Alex challenges Caiden. "Raptors or Lakers?"

"Raptors."

Alex nods. "Kawhi or LeBron?"

"LeBron for sure," Caiden says, confident in his answer.

"Okay. You're safe."

Caiden's face lights up with a smile.

"For now," Alex says pointedly, giving Caiden a menacing stare.

"These cookies are fantastic!" Mom says, impressed.

"Caiden made them," Ashley says, a hint of adoration in her voice.

I direct my attention to Caiden. "You like to bake?"

"Yeah, I do." A small smile grew on his face.

Alex smirks, clearly thinking that baking is a woman's job. Try telling that to Gordon Ramsey. I'm sure he'd give you an earful.

I take particular joy in pinching Alex hard, and he winces.

We thank the Alshaaers for a lovely evening and head back home.

CHAPTER 5

Caiden:

I KNOW WHAT YOU'RE probably thinking, 'What man in their right mind would ever step foot into a karaoke bar? Isn't that a girl thing?' Maybe. But honestly, it might be kind of fun—don't knock it until you try it.

The karaoke bar is nicely decorated with cool ultraviolet purple lights, and metallic black pendant light fixtures hang from the ceiling, casting a golden glow throughout the place. The walls are beautifully covered with music lyrics.

We walk to the booths and flip through the thick book on the desk containing the song list.

"Alright, ladies and gentlemen, this is how it's going to go: Girls vs. Guys. May the odds ever be in your favour because we are bound to win." Violet says to all of us. "Rain and Alex will be our unbiased judges."

This is going to be fun. I'm actually excited.

"Uhm, says who?" Jake says. "Wait till you see our killer moves!" He does the moonwalk as if to show that the guy's team will be bringing home the trophy tonight.

"I'll be the judge of that." Alex grins.

Across from me, Rain urges Athena not to embarrass her, like that could ever happen. Something tells me that the girls are going to beat the guys by a landslide. Athena, Violet & Vanessa team up to get ready for the battle. Melanie votes to be the videographer.

"What's with the black outfits?" Damon questions, gesturing to the girls all dressed in black. "Whose funeral is it?" He laughs.

This was not a smart move because Vanessa turns around, giving him a smoldering glare. "Yours."

Whatever happened to sweet little Vanessa?

She's long gone; Violet is definitely rubbing off on her.

· · ✿ · ·

Athena, Violet, and Vanessa waltz over to the stage to select their song. Blackpink- "Kill this love" begins to play. Everyone looks on in awe; they are killing it. Cheering them on, the girls are grinning from ear to ear. Athena looks like she is in her zone. I can't take my eyes off her and the way she floats across the stage. The song ends, and V drops the mic, pleased with their performance.

I whistle, standing up from my seat to congratulate them. "Wow, you guys are unbelievable! A force to be reckoned with."

Jake stood, clapping slowly. "I got to say, that didn't suck." Smirking, he adds, "but be prepared to lose because we play to *win*."

Jake, Damon, & I zip down our hoodies to reveal color-coordinated outfits.

Okay, before you say anything, don't judge. It's better to come prepared than to make a fool out of yourself.

Slipping on my black sunglasses, I nod to the guys who are ready to go. Athena's eyes flicker my way, taking in our ridiculously cool outfits.

I wink at her, then walk off onto the karaoke stage.

Eric Nam- "Maniac" bursts through the speakers. We gave it our all, none of us were exactly naturals at song and dance, but we tried our best. Out of all of us, though, Damon is the better dancer, so everyone followed his lead as this contagious dynamic energy flowed through us onstage.

"Now, for the moment you have all been waiting for. We decide the winners." Rain and Alex exchange a look. "My fellow judge and I will take a minute to discuss," Alex says.

With shifty eyes and nervous jitters, the only thing left to do is wait. An eternity passes before Alex and Rain walk back in, and Alex announces, "drumroll, please." Rain happily obliges and drums the tabletop.

"The winner of today's karaoke challenge goes to..." Rain trails off, looking at the anxious faces of everyone in the room.

"Just tell us already! The suspense is killing me!" Jake cries, feeling just as anxious as everyone else must be feeling.

Alex grabs the mic from Rain. "The guys!! With Manic by Eric Nam!!"

The girls look slightly disappointed at first, but then I brighten when Athena congratulates me with a warm smile. The guys are ecstatic, jumping up and down from all the excitement. The girls applaud as Rain reluctantly hands us our trophy.

I really didn't expect to win. I thought for sure the girls were a shoo-in.

The night ends on a high note. To end it off right, we decide to sing a group song. After much debate, the gang finally agreed on "Good 4 U" by Olivia Rodrigo.

Dancing and singing like a complete fool, I feel alive and carefree, enjoying every second of it.

CHAPTER 6
Caiden:

"ARE YOU SURE IT'S OKAY?" Damon asks, not sounding too convinced that it would be okay for him to leave early on such a busy day like today.

"Yeah, it's fine, don't worry. Go make sure everything is okay at home. I'll take over from here."

Damon has a mix of relief and guilt painted over his face. "I'm so sorry, man. I really owe you big time." He starts to take off, then turns back, hesitant to leave.

Clapping him on the back, I assure him with a smile that I will be just fine.

I bend down to grab the tools to take over where Damon left off. The door chimes as more customers walk in, and I assure them I'll be right with them and ask if they would please take a seat in the waiting area.

One toddler gets a little fussy, and his Mom flushes with embarrassment as she tries to calm him down. The little boy looks tired and frustrated from having to sit and wait for so long.

I rush to the front desk dresser, pulling out a colouring book and some pencil crayons. I ask his Mom for permission first to give them to him; she readily agrees and thanks me for such a sweet gesture.

The boy's eyes light up, and he's ecstatic as he takes them from me and starts colouring.

His Mom chastises Alec for having no manners, so he immediately stops what he's doing to hug me.

Peering up at me, Alec says, "Thank you." He smiles, revealing a gap between his two front teeth, which is adorable.

. . ᴏᴌᴏ . .

Everyone waited so patiently, which is a huge help, so as a courtesy, I hand out drinks to everyone on their way out. When the last customer leaves, I close the garage door, pulling the metal chain to close, and then lock it shut. I stretch my sore muscles; my shoulders and feet ache from being on my feet all day, but I simply shrug it off. It's not the first time I've worked overtime.

Lifting my face skyward, I take note of the dark clouds hovering in the evening sky. It will rain soon.

A perfect day to watch a movie.

I decide to make a quick stop at the bookstore on my way home.

. . ᴏᴌᴏ . .

I thumb through the many rows of books until I find what I am looking for.

My eyes flicker over to the black-and-white picture of Audrey Hepburn on the cover of the movie entitled "Charade."

Perfect, it's just the one I was looking for.

Mom will be so surprised since this is the *one* movie she was missing from her Audrey Hepburn collection. When I was younger, I accidentally ruined it and have yet to make it up to her.

I hope Mom likes it.

. . ᴏᴌᴏ . .

I am not usually home this early, but I wanted to give Mom some company. I've realized that over the past couple of weeks, I have been busier than usual and neglected to spend time together.

As I make my way up to the front door, my smile fades when I hear something. Turning the knob, I slowly open the door and can now make out the sound of someone sobbing. Quietly, I creep down the hallway to follow the sound.

That's when I see Mom hunched over on the ground, crying her eyes out, clutching Dad's favorite red sweater in her hands.

A surge of guilt rushes through me as my body goes stiff.

"I did this to her." My voice comes out as a whisper. "She's like this because of me."

My hands ball up into fists, and I storm off, heading to the garage. Grabbing a wrench, I slide under the car, but the wrench just falls from my trembling hand. I retrieve it, throwing the wrench across the room, watching it bounce off the brick wall before crashing to the floor.

Crouching on my knees, I close my eyes and count to 10. Luna, sensing my pain, waddles over to comfort me.

"Hey, are you okay?"

Startled, my eyes fly open.

Athena looks at me with such kindness in her eyes.

"What's that?" I motion to the glass Tupperware in her hands.

"Oh, my Mom baked these cookies and said I should bring some over for you guys." Athena rests the cookies on the hood of the car.

"Are you... okay?" Athena asks again.

Looking down at my hands, I can only mutter a reply. "I..." Taking a deep breath, I try my best to get the words out. "Sometimes... I just don't even know."

Athena keeps looking at me with her soft brown eyes.

I heave a heavy sigh, feeling the weight of the world on my shoulders. "I just feel like... I'm drowning. Gasping for air with no way out."

I look up at her now as she walks over to sit beside me on the concrete garage floor. Athena reaches over and places her hand on my knee as if to say, 'it'll be okay.'

But sadly, it's not okay, and honestly, I'm not sure that it ever will be.

CHAPTER 7

Athena:

THE DOOR CHIMES AS someone walks into the salon. "Welcome to Mia Bella's Hair Salon," I greet her before realizing who it is.

"Ashely?"

"Hi Athena, I didn't know you worked here." Ashley smiles over at me.

"I just got transferred here recently, actually. What can I help you with today?"

"I would love to colour my greys. They are showing my age."

"Sure thing."

Ashley takes a seat as I wrap the black cape around her. "Some things never change." She says with a smile on her face.

I make eye contact with her, wondering what she means by that.

"This is our favourite hair salon. We would always bring the kids here when they needed a haircut. That picture over there on the wall is one of Isabella's drawings." Ashley points over to the painting of a beautiful sunset.

"The works of an artist," I say, admiring the gorgeous array of colors capturing the beauty of the sunset perfectly.

"Yeah, she really loves to draw, but she is so self-conscious about it, we had to beg her to let them hang it up. The manager at the time loved it so much and asked if she could use it."

"Aww, that's so sweet." I mixed the grey tub of hair dye.

"This is going to feel a little cold," I say, applying the dye to her hair in small sections.

We let it sit for a bit, and Ashley continues to tell me more about what Isabella and Caiden were like growing up.

"Isabella begged every day to get a dog. We refused, thinking we were not sure if we would be able to afford one. But then, one day, our neighbor had puppies, these adorable Alaskan Klee kai puppies. One look at her and we could not resist. Since Caiden and Isabella thought she resembled the moon, we named her Luna. Although initially, she was for Isabella..." she laughs a little.

"Luna just *loves* Caiden. Luna follows him everywhere, and of course, he spoils her. Along with Isabella and me. He is such a sweetheart."

Her eyes crinkled at the corners as she claps her hands together gleefully. "How about you come over to my place for some cookies?" Ashley turned around in her chair to face me. "Caiden keeps baking up a storm, and I can't be the one to eat it all. You'd have to start rolling me out the door."

Laughing, I say, "That's ridiculous. You look amazing. Luckily for you, my shift is done, and I can't say no to dessert."

$$\bullet \bullet \sim\!\!\!\infty\!\!\!\sim \bullet \bullet$$

We leave the salon, and since we both brought our cars, we agree to meet up at her place. The drive to the Alshaaers' house from here is short, only ten minutes away.

As soon as I arrive, Luna greets me at the door, resting her fluffy paw on the glass screen.

What a cutie.

Luna waddles right up to me, and I take that as a cue to mean it's okay to pet her.

"Come on in." Ashley ushers me in as I'm still standing at the front door.

The smell of freshly baked cookies fills the air. Walking in, I notice the things I didn't pay much attention to the last time I was here. Ashley's house has such a modern feel to it. It's simple and classy, with small pops of colour that add a nice touch.

I'm in love with the mustard yellow armchair. It reminds me of the golden sun as it sets. I plop right into it, satisfied that it is equally beautiful as it is comfortable. Looks can be deceiving. Nothing is more disappointing than when something looks comfortable until you sit in it and realize it isn't. Or when you get all excited to stomp on a leaf to hear that satisfying crunch, but to your dismay, it's not a crunchy leaf. It's just wet and soggy.

Luna plops over beside me and sits comfortably on the armrest.

"You two have something in common. That's also Luna's favourite chair." Ashley hands me a plate of cookies. They are almond cookies, soft and chewy, with an almond delicately placed in the center. Yum. These are some of my all-time favourites. Glancing over by the TV, I notice Ashley has a collection of black and white movies.

"Nothing beats the classics," Ashley says, walking over to go through them before handing them to me.

"You've got quite a few Audrey Hepburn movies," I point out.

"Are you also a fan of Audrey?" Ashley asks, her eyes wide with excitement.

I really love that exactly how she feels is what shows up on her face.

"I've actually never watched one of her movies."

Ashley's jaw immediately falls open, so I clarify. "I mean, I've always wanted to but didn't get a chance to watch one yet."

"No. No. No. No. We have got to fix that." Ashley shakes her head disapprovingly. "If you're up to it, how about we watch one now?" I nod in agreement, and Ashley is overjoyed.

Something tells me we are going to get along just great.

We agree Roman Holiday would be a good choice for my first Audrey Hepburn experience. The movie plays, and right off the bat, Ashley knows every single line. I'm fascinated, not just by the movie, but by how well we get along.

· · ~ಳಿ~ · ·

Isabella bursts through the door in a frenzy, with Caiden walking in behind her. "I can't believe this!"

"What's wrong, sweetie?" Ashley asks as Isabella throws herself on the stairs in despair.

Caiden shows Ashley the test score in his hand. Isabella got a C in science, and she clearly is not pleased. "I tried hard, but I don't understand why I can't understand science," Isabella cries.

"Don't worry, Is, we can talk to your teacher and see if we can help to get your grade up. Maybe we could even get you a tutor," Caiden reassures Isabella, patting her on the back.

"If you want, I could maybe tutor her," I offer, hoping to cheer Isabella up.

Isabella lights up at that.

"That would be a fantastic idea!" Ashley beams. "It would just be until December or so until she can get her grade back up. Are you sure it won't be much trouble?"

"No, of course not. I loved taking science in school, and I'd be more than happy to tutor her," I assure her with a smile.

Isabella runs over, hugging me. "Thank you! Thank you! Thank you! You are the best!"

· · ~ಳಿ~ · ·

Caiden, being the gentleman that he is, offers to walk with me to my car.

"Well, this is me," I say as we reach the car.

"Nice car."

"Thank you," I reply. He stands there, rubbing his hand on the back of his neck.

It's quiet as we linger, waiting for each other to say something.

"Alright, so I'm going to go..." I fish for my keys in my bag. Oh, right, they are in my jacket pocket. Finding them, I press the button on the keys to open the car.

Caiden grabs my elbow to stop me from walking away. "Hey... um..."

I fixed my eyes on his hand on my elbow. He notices and pulls it away. "I, uh... didn't get to thank you... for the other day." Caiden is looking at me now, a warm smile on his face. "Thank you for being a good friend."

"You're welcome." I smile in return.

He opens his arms as if to hug me. Panicking, I raise my arms but give him two high fives instead.

The corner of his mouth turns up in something close to a smirk or a half-smile. Like he's fighting the urge to laugh.

"Well, now that I've made it awkward, I think it's about time for me to leave," I say, starting to walk away.

Idiot.

I curse to myself as soon as I am out of his sight.

I slam my head against the steering wheel, completely mortified. As I pull out, I reluctantly check my rear-view mirror to see him still standing there.

I instantly regret looking back when I see that he's looking back at me with a lopsided grin on his face.

CHAPTER 8

Athena:

"OKAY, LET'S GO OVER the steps one more time," Violet says as she bends down to retie her shoelaces.

We are at the dance studio—one of our favourite places. I roll my eyes, but of course, she can see me in the huge 10-foot mirror. She tends to be—I apologize for the lack of a better word—bossy. Nonetheless, I continue to put up with it because she puts up with me. And trust me when I say I can be a bit of a handful at times.

"Yes, ma'am!" I shout, saluting like a soldier getting ready for battle. Violet pushes me in response, so I jump on her back and tackle her.

"I swear if you don't stop practicing those self-defense moves on me, one of these days I will kill you," Violet says, a hint of annoyance in her voice.

"Be sure to hide the evidence." I flash her a teasing grin. "Do it nice and cleanly, so it doesn't leave a trace."

"Oh, don't worry. I already have it all planned out. I'll pin it all on your brother. Everyone will think he had it out for you all this time, so it was only a matter of time."

I ponder on it for a moment. "Yep, pretty believable."

· · ⌇⌇ · ·

We head home exhausted. Reaching for my phone, I realize I must have left it at the studio. I call the dance studio, asking them if they see it to please give me a call on the house phone.

At least, I *hope* that's where I left it. I can be a little absent-minded at times.

"Is nobody going to get the phone?" Rain calls out from upstairs.

Colour me surprised.

No one ever wants to answer the phone. I don't see why we even still have it; I mean, we all have cell phones.

Even Sky has a cell phone.

Oh wait, maybe it's the studio, and they found my phone.

Flying down the stairs to answer it, I pick it up but realize it's not for me. Someone else already answered it. Mom's voice is on the other end. She must be talking to one of her friends. Oh, how she loves to socialize. She is a social butterfly.

I'm about to put the phone back down when I hear his voice. An all too familiar one that I haven't heard in years. A cold chill runs up my spine when the realization kicks in.

That's Dad's voice.

How do I even begin to process all of this? My mind is spiraling, and my throat tightens as breathing becomes harder. I need to get out of here.

I grab my swimsuit and goggles, and I don't even pause to say bye as I charge out the door. Sky's in the living room, completely content watching TV while eating chips. I'm sure no one will even notice when I leave. Slamming the door for good measure, my feet lead the way, already knowing where I want to go—my retreat and safe haven, the beach.

.. ᴼᵒ ..

The waves crash onto the quiet sun-bleached sand. Leaping downward through the air, I plunge into the water, gliding through the vast ocean. My breath flows throughout my body, giving my arms and legs the power to stroke and kick. I watch the light playing amid the currents in shining whites, blues, and rainbow colours.

• • ⁓ • •

As I trudge my way back to the house, I'm physically and mentally exhausted. All I want to do is stretch my sore muscles and hop into the shower.

It makes me mad that I'm even angry. That even after all these years, I'm still letting him have this hold over me. But that fact doesn't calm the fire burning within me. Emotions are a funny thing. No matter how far down you bury them, they always seem to find a way to climb back up to the surface. No matter how much you would love to keep those feelings buried.

When I walk back into the house, I can sense that something is off. The air has shifted; something is wrong. Collin tells me that Alex stormed off when he found out who Mom was on the phone with. Collin didn't quite understand why, as he doesn't know the whole story. He says that he and Mom haven't had a chance to talk about it yet.

It is now close to midnight, and Alex still isn't back yet. Knowing Alex, the only place he would stay out this late is at the gym. I'm so going to kill him when I see him. How dare he just run off like that, staying out all night without having the decency to tell anyone where he is going? So irresponsible.

• • ⁓ • •

Lo-and-behold, there he is, boxing away like he's got no cares in the world. He obviously sees me because he meets my eye and then immediately looks away. I walk over to him, and Alex ignores me as he fiercely pounds his fist into the punching bag.

Crossing my arms, I call him out. Running away doesn't fix anything. "You can't just dismiss the problem and act like it's not there." It's fine to need some time to yourself to process things, but he can't just hide out here forever. "Ignoring it doesn't make it disappear. When exactly are you going to grow up and—"

"Oh, you mean like *you* do?"

"Excuse me?"

"You shut everyone out, Athena. You don't tell anyone how you actually feel. So, you don't have the right to stand here and act all high and mighty. At the very least, you should be honest with yourself."

Fuming with the anger, I spit back, "You know, you have your whole life to be a jerk. Why not just take today off? And for the record, you have no idea what you are talking about. You think you know me, but you don't."

CHAPTER 9
Athena:

WE ARE ON A ROLL. THE tutoring is going great so far, and Isabella is really starting to understand this.

Isabella's getting all the answers right, but for some reason, she doesn't seem too pleased. Her mind is somewhere else. "Hey, is everything okay?"

"Hm? Yeah, I'm fine."

"Okay, but if you ever want to talk about something," I say while giving her a reassuring smile, "or need a listening ear, I'm here for you."

Isabella brightens a little. Sighing, she says, "Can I ask you a question?"

"Of course, go ahead."

"What do you do when someone is picking on you?" Isabella asks, sounding self-conscious.

Tapping my chin for a moment, I ask her, "Is this someone, a girl or a boy?"

"A boy. Ezra doesn't stop picking on me and calling me names."

I nod, knowing exactly how she feels. "I've been in this situation before. It really sucks, doesn't it?"

Isabella's mouth hangs open. "No way! Someone had the nerve to bully *you*? I am shocked."

I laugh. "When I was about your age, I was a lot quieter, and I guess that made people think I was easy to pick on."

"Unbelievable." Isabella looks up at me, her eyes wide with wonder.

"His name was Cordell. Each day he made it his aim to make me miserable. He'd pick apart my face saying I looked like a frog and shouldn't smile because it only made me uglier."

"How dare he!"

"Yeah, it was not one of my fondest memories of middle school, but you know what helped?"

"What?"

"Back then, my dad asked me if any of the accusations he made about me were actually true. I said no. Then, he told me that if someone says an insult, but I know it isn't true, then I shouldn't let it bother me. Because he's wrong," I tell her.

Isabella blinks for a moment, considering this possibility.

"And you know what else he told me?" I go on, "That more than likely Cordell actually liked me.

That was the real reason he paid so much attention to me."

Isabella's shaking her head. "That's ridiculous. Who bullies the person who they like?"

"I know. It makes absolutely no sense. Us girls, we are smarter than that. But guys tend to be pretty stupid sometimes."

Isabella laughs. "So, was it true? *Did* he like you?" she asks, propping up on her knees.

"Once we got to high school. His whole demeanor changed. He started smiling at me and would try to talk to me and was actually... nice to me. It was strange. And then my best friend at the time told me that Cordell told him he liked me."

"Wow, that's crazy."

"Yep. Crazy that my dad was actually right."

Isabella's quiet for a moment. "But weren't you scared to tell your dad in case he went and made it worse?"

"At first, yes. But then we made a compromise. He wouldn't come to the school or go to Cordell's house because that would embarrass me and only make matters worse. But he said that the minute Cordell laid a hand on me, he wouldn't back down. So, if that ever happened, which he hoped wouldn't, I would have to let him handle it. Otherwise, he promised to let me deal with it on my own."

Isabella pulls at the skin around her fingers. "I want to tell Caiden and Mom about it, but not unless it's absolutely necessary. So they don't have to worry about me. Could you keep this a secret, just between us?"

"Tell you what; I'll keep a secret but only if you promise to keep me updated on what happens. But if he lays a finger on you at any time, I will have to say something. Deal?"

"Deal." Isabella extends her hand, and I shake it.

Caiden:

LITTLE DO THEY KNOW I am standing behind Isabella's door listening in on their private conversation. Maybe I should feel at least a tad bit guilty about it, but as Isabella's older brother, I couldn't resist. The second I find this Ezra kid, I'm going to give him a good stern... talking to so he knows who he's messing with.

The doorknob rattles.

I scramble over to the kitchen, ducking for cover. Act natural, I remind myself. Athena and Isabella open the door to find me sitting awkwardly at the dining table reading a book.

"Hey, guys." I try my best to keep my expression neutral.

"Pride and Prejudice, interesting choice," Isabella notes.

"Well, you know... it's a classic. Best love story ever told... you know, after Romeo and Juliet?"

Isabella raises an eyebrow. "You mean the one where they *died* in the end?"

Ah, no, I take that back now. "Yeah, no, the other one with the better ending."

"Uh-huh."

Athena's clearly enjoying this; she is fake coughing into her sleeve, trying to disguise holding back a laugh.

I feel like I am visibly sweating profusely. "I'm going to go uh... go outside... you know, to read while enjoying some nice fresh air." This is exactly why I can't lie. I'm horrible at it.

I scamper off, grateful to be out of there.

. . ⚭ . .

"Is that a 1996 Shelby 427 Cobra?" Athena asks. I'm pleasantly surprised to see that she came to join me outside, or at least that's what I'm *hoping* she came outside for.

She runs over to glide her hand over the hood of the car, admiring it.

"Yeah." A questioning look played on my face. "How did you—"

"Let's just say I know a thing or two about cars."

You never cease to amaze me, I think to myself. Out loud, I tell her, "We really need to talk more."

"Why?"

"Because... you're cool, and I like talking to you."

"Okay, then, let's talk." Athena smiles that radiant smile of hers. "What do you want to know?"

"Everything." I clarify by saying, "within reason, of course. If there's anything off-limits, you could say... bananas."

"Bananas?"

I give her a broad smile. "Yes, just go with it." I clasp my hands together, joining to stand beside her.

"Who's first?"

Athena puts her hands out in front of us, initializing rock paper scissors. "Best two out of three?"

"Deal. Winner gets to go first."

Athena wins the first round, but I win the next two, granting me the honor of going first. "What's your most embarrassing childhood memory?" I ask her, curious.

"My friends and I were playing basketball in our backyard. I ran back in to get water, and I guess I was so excited to get back to the game that I ran through the screen door, not realizing it wasn't open. So, I went *flying*, and the screen popped off and went sailing with me." Athena hangs her head in shame.

"What-"

I laughed so hard I thought I might topple over. "How..." I say, clutching my stomach. "How could you *not* see the door?"

Athena shrugs, smiling at me before she starts laughing too. She continues by saying that they never let her live it down. Anytime someone played basketball with her, it would be brought up again.

After a good laugh, Athena asks the next one. "What's something you enjoy but would refuse to admit if asked?"

"Musicals. That, and I've watched high school musicals one, two, and three at least..."—I pause to count on my fingers—"30 times now."

Athena laughs at my confession. "30?"

I nod, smiling proudly. Okay, so the first time, I was suckered into watching it for Isabella, but then it turned out that I didn't hate it as much as expected.

"Now *that's* an accomplishment," Athena says, sounding impressed.

"Why, thank you." I proceed to bow over dramatically, causing her to giggle. I like the sound of her laugh. "Who do you take after more? Your Mom or your Dad?"

"According to Mom, I'm a different breed, but I look a lot like my dad." She pauses for a moment. "The truth is, I have two dads. Collin is my stepdad. My biological dad and I... aren't exactly on speaking terms right now. He's my dad in name only."

I listen empathetically. I can tell that talking about her father isn't easy for her. "Oh, I didn't know that. I just assumed Collin was your real dad. I guess because you guys seem so close."

"We are." Her face brightens a little. "Collin is a great stepdad." She says. "With my dad, it's... complicated." Athena wraps a piece of her hair that fell out of her ponytail around her finger. She seems to want to steer the topic of conversation away from her relationship with her biological father.

"What's your biggest regret?" Athena asks next, directing her attention back to me.

I look over the Shelby parked in the garage. Rubbing a hand along my jaw, I opt to skip out on this one. "Bananas."

Athena nods, not pushing the matter further or asking any follow-up questions. Although I could tell she probably wanted to. I'm quiet for a bit, then turn to face her, conflicted about whether I should say what's on my mind.

"Hey, um... if you don't mind me saying, I hope I'm not overstepping in any way... because, of course, I don't know what happened, but if there's anything I've come to learn in my experience, it's that you don't want to wait until it is too late. The regret... might just eat you up inside."

There's an expression on her face that I can't quite figure out. Oh great, I blew it. She must be mad. "I'm sorry. I didn't mean to—"

Athena waves a hand. "No, it's fine. I appreciate your honesty. I'm not mad."

"Well... since we're on the topic of honesty. I should probably tell you... I kind of overheard your conversation with Isabella about the bully."

"How much did you hear?"

"Just the part about Cordell and some Ezra kid that dared to bully my sister. If he ever lays a hand on her, I swear I'll-"

"Easy there. That's precisely why she didn't tell you." Athena smiles at me. "Don't worry. I'll keep an eye on her and let you know if anything happens."

I smile at her, thinking I'm glad Isabella has someone to talk to. "Thank you for taking care of her."

CHAPTER 10

Athena:

A TEXT FROM MEL APPEARS on my phone screen.

Mel: Hey girl. 7 o'clock tonight, games night at my place.
Athena: Sounds great!

I scurry to the kitchen, where Mom and Colin sit at the kitchen table.

"Why hello, my lovely daughter," Collin greets me with a big smile. Seeing the look on my face, Mom puts down her coffee mug as Collin, reading my mind, asks what's up.

I excitedly ramble on about Violet's friend Mel, who invited me to games night tonight at her place today.

"Sounds like fun, why don't you bring Rain & Alex with you?" Mom asks.

My smile instantly fades.

"You have got to be kidding me," I say, suddenly horrified at what my night will turn out to be.

Bringing them along was definitely *not* a part of the plan.

Marching into Alex's room, I shake his shoulders to wake him up. He doesn't budge, so I kick him. "Hey, what are you kicking me for?" Alex says, squinting his eyes at me.

"Well, maybe if you had woken up the first time I tried to wake you, I wouldn't have had to kick you. We are going to a game night tonight. Go get ready. We leave in 20 minutes."

"Will there be food?"

"Duh."

Classic Alex.

I close his bedroom door, shaking my head. Alex sleeps the day away, and all he cares about is food. Well, I guess he might enjoy the luxury while he can.

Banging on the bathroom door, I tell Rain to hurry up. "You are not going to make me late! If you're not in the car in 20 minutes, you're not going!"

"You mean, *you're* not."

"I don't have the time or patience to deal with you right now." I pinch the bridge of my nose, annoyed. "Let's go!"

"Hey, it's not my fault your life is a mess." Rain yells back.

．． ∽ ．．

In the car on the way to Mel's, I sneak a glance at Alex. Rain is glued to her phone screen, headphones on, bobbing her head to the music.

"I want you to be friends with someone." I was careful to keep my voice light and casual.

Alex eyes me from the passenger seat. "You do realize that now that you want me to, I'm not going to, right?"

"Yes, but couldn't you just do it *because* I'm asking you to?"

"Who is it?"

I hesitate before answering. "Caiden."

"Why?"

I'm starting to wonder why I even brought this up. Well. The cat's already out of the bag, might as well follow through with it. "Seriously? Do you really need me to spell it out to you? I thought you were smarter than that."

"Listen, I'm still half-asleep. I just got up. Spit it out."

I can't believe I'm doing this; I don't dare to look at Alex. I keep my eyes focused on the road ahead of me. "Because I want to be friends with him, and I'd like it if you were friends or at least okay with him. You don't have to be *best* friends or whatever."

"How old is he?"

Caiden is two years older than me.

"Twenty-one."

"You know you're going to regret telling me this."

"I figured as much."

Alex nodded firmly. "I'm going to kill him."

"What, why? It's not like he even hit on me or anything. Relax."

"Either way, I'm going to kill him."

"Could you relax? That won't be necessary."

. . ⚬ɸ⚬ . .

We arrive at Mel's place, and as soon as I put the car in park, Alex opens the car door. "Bye."

I have a million and one questions about what just happened here. How in the world did that escalate so fast? Funny enough, I was pleasantly surprised at first by how well he was taking it—not overreacting as usual. And then... Alex did what Alex always does—he flew off the handle.

Well, that's to be expected.

I trail in behind Rain and Alex, walking down to the basement where Mel is hosting her game night. Mel has a really nice, finished basement. It is decorated with light grey walls and white furniture. Fairy lights wrapped around the stair railings and posts.

"Perfect timing. Now that everyone is here, we can play two truths and a lie. For any of you who don't know the game, this is how it goes." Mel looks around to make sure everyone is paying attention and then continues, "We each write three sentences about ourselves. Two are the truth, and one is a lie. We will ask you questions to help determine what we think it might be. Any questions?"

Jake raises his hand, which earns him a few laughs from his audience.

"You'll just have to catch up," Mel says half-heartedly.

Violet goes up first.

There is a glimmer of mischief on her face. Out of all of us, I'm pretty sure she has the best poker face.

Violet holds up three envelopes and asks us which one we want to pick, envelope A, B, or C.

"Envelope A seems like a good choice, right guys?" Nessa asks us.

"I don't know. Look at the way Violet's holding B, so limp and lifeless, like she doesn't want us to choose it. But what if that's a part of her plan,"—Jake pauses for emphasis—"and she really wants us to choose A?" He taps his chin.

Alex grabs envelope A out of Violet's hands. "I guess there's only one way to find out." Ripping it open, the words inside the paper read, "I can touch my nose with my tongue." We all openly stare at her while we huddle up together, strategizing.

"Stick out your tongue," Mel declares.

Violet does as she is told, which is quite unusual for her.

"I don't think she is sticking it out all the way... unless she is! And it's a lie!" Jake says to Violet.

"Is that your final answer?" Violet asks.

Jake turns to Nessa. "Permission to state my case, your honor?"

Nessa nods. "Granted."

"Okay, we need to strategize here. Everyone stick out your tongue," Jake says. As weird as a request that is, we all oblige.

"Okay, let's see here..." Jake walks around, examining all of us.

"One more for the archives." Seizing the opportunity, Rain clicks a photo of me with my tongue hanging out.

"Cut it out." I gesture with an 'I'm going to kill you' slit to the throat.

"Alex, touch your nose," Caiden says.

"Okay, easy." Alex tries his best but struggles to follow through.

We laugh at his failed attempt. "Give me a minute. I've got it," Alex says.

"Ahhhh." Jake mimics the sound of the buzzer from America's Got Talent. "Next!" He goes around again, questioning whether or not Violet's confession could be the truth or a lie.

"Alright, the verdict is in. Permission to speak, your honor?" Jake asks Nessa.

"Granted."

Jake clears his throat. "It is... a lie." He looks at Violet to see her reaction.

"Okay," Violet says simply. Just like that, no indication as to whether we suspected right or wrong.

Dang, she is good.

• • ⚘ • •

To mix things up a bit, up next are me, Mel, and Nessa. To make it more challenging, this round will be multiple choice. There will be a total of five *true and false* statements. But the trick is we have to decide which statement belongs to *who*.

The statements are:

I can touch my nose with my tongue.

I have eaten the world's stinkiest cheese.

I had my first beer when I was five.

I am a proud member of the grammar police.

I once shaved my brother's leg while he was sleeping.

"Look at those beady eyes. She seems like the secret alcoholic type," Alex implies, pointing to Nessa.

"Mm. Mm." Drew agrees.

"I shaved my brother's leg while he was sleeping. That's a good one. Alex shows us your legs, man." Caiden prods him.

"I'm suddenly feeling so exposed," Alex says, covering himself with a blanket.

Where'd he even get a blanket? I wonder. But Alex, being well Alex, it doesn't take much for him to get what he wants.

"World's stinkiest cheese, huh? When and where?" Violet looks to me for the answer.

"Why do you assume it's me?"

"I'm not assuming anything just yet." Folding her arms across her chest, Violet continues, "Now answer my question. When and where?"

"June 25th. In France."

Violet narrows her eyes, not believing it. "What year?"

"2011," I reply.

"Ah, I see you picked when I was away at school, clever." Violet asks, "Do you have pictures from said trip?"

"Yes, ma'am." I confidently hold up my phone and scroll through the photos as evidence.

"Wait a minute. Let me see those," Alex says, examining my phone.

"Mhm, just as I thought. These are photoshopped," Alex says definitively.

"I object," Jake chimes in. He grabs a chair and plops it right in front of me, looking me straight in the eye. "What did it taste like?"

"It tastes like a perfectly normal, sweet brie with a massively bitter aftertaste."

"Okay, Siri, what's the name of the stinkiest cheese in the world, and how does it taste?" Siri recites back word for word exactly what I say.

Well, now I'm going to seem a whole lot less convincing.

"Aha! Just as I suspected. Google copy and paste." Jake brushes invisible dirt off his hands. "Alright, it's a wrap here. Case closed."

Jake turns to face everyone. "I think we can all agree on the following conclusions. Violet can't touch her nose with her tongue, even though she's bold and daring enough to do it."

"You." Jake points at Nessa, and she looks surprised.

"Yes, you. Do not give me those innocent eyes. You're a drinker." Jake then turns his attention to Mel. "Okay, grammar police. We're going to go ahead and give that one to Mel. She plays tough, but deep inside, I bet she's a total nerd."

Jake smiles at me. "Last but not least is Athena. She put up a good fight. You almost had me going there, but you've been caught. You did not try the world's stinkiest cheese, but I believe you wanted to."

I smirk, thinking he has no idea what really happened here, but he will soon find out.

"Why is she making up her face like that? Did I get it wrong?" Jake panics.

Violet speaks up now. "Contestants, please reveal the answers." We hold up the papers, revealing the correct answers.

I ate the world's stinkiest cheese - Violet.

I was a member of the grammar police – Athena.

I can touch my nose with my tongue - Nessa.

I had my first beer when I was five – Mel.

Alex and Jake are appalled.

"How could you? You guys teamed up to trick us, didn't you?" Jake crosses his arms.

"Well..." Nessa starts.

We did indeed decide to team up and see if we could get the guys to believe our made-up stories about the trip I did actually go on, but I did *not* try the world's stinkiest cheese. It was Violet who did, and it worked.

"That was so much fun. A, your poker face was phenomenal." Violet high-fives me.

"Thank you, thank you." I bow.

.. ∾⟡∾ ..

Mel clasps her hands together. "And now, for the last game of the night, nighttime has fallen. Close your eyes."

"Don't tell me to close my eyes. You don't get to tell me what to do," Jake whines.

Mel gives him a side-eye, and Jake clams up. "Yes, ma'am."

Jake rubs his hands together. "If anyone's feeling generous, save me, please, I beg of you."

Mel silences him. "Shh, no talking." Jake whimpers.

Poor guy, my guess is he will be the first one to die.

"Morning has come," Mel announces. We all open our eyes.

Mel glances over in Jake's direction. "Okay, what did I do now?" Jake asks.

"What?"

"You look like you want to rip my head off," Jake replies.

"Sorry, that's just how my face works." Mel shrugs.

Mel clears her throat. "We have had an unfortunate death among us. Someone here just happened to speak at the wrong moment. He walked into the convenience store, wondering why it was so quiet, and called out for anyone that worked there. Bang! The sniper pulled the trigger, and now he's *dead*."

"Wow, that's so unfortunate. It was nice knowing you, buddy." Caiden puts an arm around Jake.

"Wait, hold up. Why are you assuming it's *me*?" Jake looks around, and we're all giving him pitiful stares.

"I'm sorry, Jake, but you are now dead," Mel says sadly.

"Hold on a second. None of you ever *tried* to save me? Wow, I need some new friends. Some friends you are." Jake paces back and forth, annoyed. "You know what? I'm glad to be dead. I'd like to take a good look at my killer."

Alex stares long and hard at me before declaring, "Athena's the mafia."

I blink.

How dare he-

"See how quiet she is? *Definitely* the mafia." Alex leans back in his chair with his arms crossed, examining me.

Jake gasps. "I feel betrayed."

"No, Jake, I would never!" I plead.

"Shall we take a vote?" Mel asks. "Alright. Who votes Athena as the mafia?"

Everyone, *including* Violet, put their hands up.

Traitor.

"Jake, put your hand down. Dead people don't vote," Mel says, and Jake lowers his hand.

I'm silent as I watch all the hands go up. Caiden smiles sympathetically, and I smile back.

Caiden's the only one who didn't vote me off.

The game continues, and still, no one has guessed who the other mafia is—assuming I was one of the mafias, of course.

"My bets are on Violet. If I die this round, she is the mafia. We all know she's been trying to kill me since the day she met me," Alex says.

Violet stares at Alex. "Well, don't give me a reason to kill you then."

"You see that?!" Alex points at Violet. "She is trying to avenge Athena's death. They are in this together!"

Violet gets voted off the island next but not without getting the last word in.

"Don't be fooled," Violet warns. "The *real* mafia is actually sitting *very* close to you."

"Nighttime has fallen," Mel narrates.

"Hold on a sec. There's still another mafia?" Alex looks worried.

He should be.

The game ensues, and to everyone's surprise, Mel tells us that the Mafia has *won* this round.

"How..." Alex scratches his head, confused. "How is that possible?"

"Easy. I was the Mafia," Rain says proudly.

"No way!" Jake is beside himself that Rain would do such a thing.

No one saw that coming. Sweet, innocent Rain no longer looks so *sweet* and *innocent*. Like I said before, it's the quiet ones you have to watch out for.

"Along with V and Athena, of course," Rain explains.

Okay, so yes, I *was* one of the Mafia's... but Alex just *had* to jump the gun, ruining it for me.

I glare at Alex.

"Why are you glaring at me?" Alex asks, oblivious as usual.

"I'm hoping you will spontaneously combust." I don't even care that there's venom and spite in my voice.

Violet tries to console me, but I'm too annoyed at Alex. "I know, I know he blew your cover. But I mean... it was bound to happen sooner or later." Shrugging, Violet says, "it just happened sooner rather than later."

"Exactly," I say, eyeing Alex, who slumps in his seat like a scared baby. "And for the record,"—I turn to face Jake—"It *wasn't* my idea to kill you, Jake. It was Rain's."

Jake nods, forgiving me.

"Why me?" Jake asks Rain, not understanding why she would hate him so much to kill him off first. "What did I ever do to you?"

A small smile tugs on the corner of Rain's lips. "You talked too much."

See what I mean about the quiet ones being silent but deadly?

Jake scrapes his chair back and stands. "Well, this was fun." His voice drips sarcasm.

"It was, wasn't it?" Rain smiles at him.

"Yes, it was *unbelievably great*. Let's *never* do this again," Jake says.

CHAPTER 11
Caiden:

ATHENA, ISABELLA, AND I are eating at the kitchen table when Isabella blurts out, "Guys, look at this!"

"What is it, Is?" I ask. Isabella turns her laptop towards us so we can see the image on the screen. She is on the 'Underwater Sea Life' home page, where it is announcing a '1 day only ticket deal'.

"Let's go to the aquarium today! I've been dying to go, and *today* only they are even having a deal. Buy two, get one *free*."

I look at Athena to see her reaction, hoping she will want to come too. "Sounds like fun," Athena says. I try not to leap out of my seat from the excitement.

Play it cool, Caiden.

"Do you want to come with us?" Like me, Isabella is at the edge of her seat, pleading with her eyes for Athena to say yes.

There's no way Athena could say no to Isabella.

Athena smiles. "I would love to."

"Yes!" Isabella jumps out of her seat, putting her dishes in the sink, all geared up and ready to go.

I suggest that since it is such a beautiful day outside, we could even bike ride over.

"That's a great idea!" Isabella says. Grabbing onto Athena's arm, Isabella tells her she can borrow Mom's bike.

Athena offers to help clean the kitchen, but there's absolutely no way I'm letting her do that.

"Guests don't clean, don't be ridiculous." I promptly take the plates from her hands.

"Fine. Let me *help* then." Athena walks to the sink and grabs the towel, tossing me the sponge. "You wash. I'll dry."

Of course, Athena's not the type to just take no for an answer. "Yes, ma'am," I say, smiling.

. . ᴏᴧ๑ . .

We wash dishes, standing side by side, and I can't help but peek at her. Smiling to myself, all I can think is that I could definitely get used to this.

Athena flicks soap suds at me. "Stop slacking off. Look how much *I* did." She gestures to the pile of dishes she has finished drying and placed neatly on the countertop.

Show off.

"For the record, *you* started this." I scoop two handfuls of soap water and dump them on her head.

Athena blinks in complete shock. Then she dips the *huge* stainless-steel bowl into the sink, filling it with soap water, a devious look on her face as she moves towards me.

"Wait, let's think about this," I say, carefully taking a few steps backward.

"Too late for that." Athena grins from ear to ear, then pours the contents of the soap water all over me.

The two of us just stand there soaking wet, dripping water all over the marble floor. Unable to help ourselves, we burst out in laughter. The sight of our messy, disheveled hair and soap suds everywhere is hilarious.

We are interrupted by the rumbling thunder and heavy rain beating against the window.

"You guys are soaked!" Isabella says, hurrying to give Athena some of Mom's clothes to wear while hers dry.

Isabella follows Athena to the laundry room, insisting that we still go to the aquarium today. "I'm not going to let a little rain rain on my parade." Isabella pouts.

"Of course not," Athena says. "We are still going."

· · ໕ · ·

We all change and get ready. Since the rain ruined our bike riding plans, Athena says we can take her car to the aquarium instead.

Dodging the big fat raindrops, I hold the umbrella for Athena and Isabella, shielding them from the rain. Isabella slides into the back seat, so I sit up front in the passenger's seat.

"Woah, I love your car. The seats are so comfy I could easily fall asleep," Isabella says, reclining the car seatback.

"Thank you. If you can fall asleep while I'm driving, I'd take that as a compliment."

Athena starts the car up, and we take off, making our way to the aquarium.

I take a deep breath.

In and out, trying to steady my heart that feels like it's going to burst right out of my chest.

Inhale...

And exhale...

It's okay.

We're fine. Everything is going to be okay, I remind myself.

Just breathe.

Athena glances at me. Her lips are moving, but I can't really make out what she is saying.

"Music..." I think I heard her say something about music.

My body feels like it's overheating, and I'm starting to sweat.

Athena touches my arm, then immediately yanks it back. "Caiden, you're burning up." She takes note of the sweat on my forehead. I self-consciously wipe it off on the side of my shirt sleeve.

"It's because it's hot outside." I try to shrug it off, hoping the strain in my voice doesn't give me away.

Athena glances at her dashboard, pointing out that it's only 10° out.

"My internal temperature is always high, so to me, it feels like 25°," I spew out a lie.

Athena tilts her head to the side, considering it. Whether or not she believes the lie, she doesn't say anything more about it.

I crack open the window, hoping some cool air will help me breathe.

. . ⚬⚭⚬ . .

Aquariums are filled with underwater sea life that many have never seen in their entire life. The creatures of the ocean are so unique and beautiful. Nothing can compare to the magnificence of seeing it in real life.

I am stocked that Isabella suggested we spend the day here.

Looking through the massive water tank in front of us, I'm mesmerized by the bright purple and lilac jellyfish. The gold plaque beside the jellyfish tank tells us that jellyfish are actually not fish at all. They have no backbone, so they *absorb* oxygen from the water from membranes, unlike fish, who live in the water and breathe *through* their gills.

Huh, who would have thought?

Even more surprising is the fact that a 505-million-year-old fossil suggests that jellyfish may even pre-date dinosaurs.

Woah.

Next, we move on to the octopus's tank. The octopus glides through the tank with ease as it dives through the deep red and blue coral reefs. The sign posted beside the tank mentions that an octopus has three hearts.

Wow. So, does that mean an octopus would feel *three* times as much as we do?

Athena observes the light pink octopus, its big beady eyes staring back at us. "Did you know that when an octopus is stressed out, it eats its arms?"

Wait, what?

"How exactly does that work?" I ask, fully invested in this now. "Do they just grow back?" Athena nods. "Yep, within a month or so, the arm will grow back."

I guess it's true. You learn something new every day.

I scroll on my phone to find the list of questions I want to ask her.

Yes, I wrote them all down.

Yes, that's weird and corny, I know, and I don't care.

"Do you believe in second chances?" I ask, curious about what her answer might be.

"No." Athena's response was immediate, like she didn't even need to give it a second thought. Nodding, I don't say anything because I'm sure she has a good reason for saying that.

"Fool me once, shame on you. Fool me twice, shame on me." Athena laughs half-heartedly. "Or at least, I'd like to think that I wouldn't be foolish enough to make the same mistake twice."

Ouch.

Someone must have really hurt her. Who could ever do such a thing?

"Wow, unbelievable."

"What?" Athena looks over at me, a questioning look playing on her face.

"I just can't wrap my head around the fact that someone would be stupid enough to do that."

"Do what?"

"Let you go," I say, smiling. Athena grins, bright and happy, and all I can think is there is nothing I would not do to keep that smile on her face.

I find myself becoming forgetful at times. When I am with her, I forget that I don't deserve to be happy.

Athena looks at me while I'm lost in thought as if she wonders what I'm thinking.

I give her a faint smile, and she clears her throat, gearing up to ask the next question. "Have you ever been unable to sleep? And, if so, what do you do with your time then?"

Yeah, all the time.

"Yeah, quite often actually, and when that happens, I need some kind of release. For me, that's pottery."

"What got you to take an interest in pottery?" Athena asks, her eyes shining.

"I think it's because... I like being in control. I hate the feeling of my life slipping between my fingers." I think back to that day in the garage, Athena looking at me with such kind eyes. That's all it took to comfort me. She always manages to do that so effortlessly.

Athena smiles at me. "Then hold on to it. You won't let it go so easy if it's that important to you."

I smile back, a look of determination in my eyes. "You're right, and I won't." With every fiber of my being, I promised myself right then and there that I won't give up.

Isabella slides in between us, shoving me away in the process. "Stop hogging her all to yourself." Isabella leans over to whisper something in Athena's ear, making her giggle.

"What's so funny?" I ease closer to them, trying to hear what they are talking about. "Tell me. I want to laugh too!"

Athena and Isabella simply ignore me, leaving me behind, following them like a lost puppy.

. . ✿ . .

Outside the aquarium, Isabella speeds over to the hill, sitting down on the grass. Luckily, I packed a blanket and some snacks for us so we could have a picnic after.

"Where's the bag with the snacks you packed for us?" I hand Isabella the snacks in the black duffel bag while I pull out the checkered red and white blanket for us to sit on, laying it on the grass.

Isabella holds up the bag of peanut M&Ms in her hand. "Who did you pack *this* for?"

Of course, she would notice that I packed that. Hopefully, she will just let this one go.

"*I* don't like peanuts, and *you* are severely allergic to peanuts. So, did you bring this for..." Isabella motions towards Athena.

"I packed them for me," I say quickly, then regret it when I realize how utterly stupid I must sound right about now. Nice one, Caiden.

"What? But you're allergic."

"No, I'm not."

"Oh, really?" Isabella raises an eyebrow. "Tell that to the hives you had all over your neck."

I shake my head, continuing with this ridiculous charade we got going here. "Well, not anymore. I outgrew it, and I am fine now."

"Mm, okay. Then go ahead and eat one."

Caught in the lie, I'm left with no other choice. "What?"

"Eat one."

I try to laugh it off like it's no big deal. "Like right now?" Isabella nods. Athena looks at us, biting the inside of her cheek to keep herself from laughing.

Yeah, okay. I can do this.

I take the bag of M&M's from Isabella, taking my sweet time opening it.

This is it.

This is how I will die.

Nope, can't do it. "This is childish."

An ice cream truck passes by, saving my sorry behind. "Oh, look! An ice cream truck." I point over to the white truck at the bottom of the hill. "Who wants ice cream?"

I've never been more grateful to see an ice cream truck in my entire life.

Athena:

ON THE DRIVE HOME, Isabella takes the front seat. She called shotgun. Since Caiden got to sit in the front seat on the way here, she insisted it was only fair.

Isabella fiddles with the radio before settling on a song by Chris Daughtry. "It's not over" starts to play, and she cranks the volume up, humming along to the music.

In the backseat of the car, Caiden starts to sing along to the song.

I was listening so intently to Caiden singing that I almost forgot where I was. The green light turns red, and I glance wide-eyed at him in my rear-view mirror.

Caiden looks surprised by my reaction. "Why are you looking at me like that?"

"You're singing that was..." I shake my head. "Unbelievably great. Your voice is incredible."

Caiden smiles awkwardly, baffled by the compliment.

CHAPTER 12
6 MONTHS LATER...
Athena:

I HAVE STARTED TO GET used to and maybe even enjoy having him... I mean, *them* around—Isabella and Caiden, that is. I find myself looking forward to spending time with them.

As I walk up to the Alshaaers' front porch, I take note of the beautiful flower basket hanging over the steel metal door. It's a mix of scarlet and fuchsia-coloured bleeding hearts. Or 'rebels' as I call them because, unlike most flowers, bleeding hearts are one of the very few that bloom upside down. I tilt my head backward to take a closer look.

Right then, the front door swings open, and Ashley is standing inside the front door. "Hello," I say, looking up at her while upside down.

Ashley laughs. Telling me to come on in, she quickly hurries over to the kitchen to fetch me something to drink.

Ashely hands me a cool glass of strawberry lemonade. "Thank you."

"I was surprised to see you here." Ashley smiles, taking a sip of her drink. "I thought you were meeting up with Caiden and Isabella at the park."

"What do you mean?"

Ashley puts down her drink. "Caiden didn't text you?"

That's weird. I don't remember Caiden or Isabella mentioning anything. As far as I knew, we were going to meet here as usual for Isabella's tutoring. I pull out my phone to check my messages. There is one unread message from Caiden. It turns out he *did* text me, saying that I should meet them at the park. But since I was driving, I am only *now* seeing this message.

That explains it.

"Don't look at the mess. I was in the middle of starting to clean up and get some laundry done." That's ridiculous. The Alshaaers' house is always so spotless. My Mom is the same; the house is never clean enough for her. Not one of us can live up to *her* standard of cleanliness.

"What mess? Your place is always so clean!" Ashley smiles at the compliment. "Since I'm here, let me help you." I stand up from the mustard yellow couch.

The two of us sort, wash, dry, and start folding all the clothes, putting them into a pile on top of the dryer.

"I can't believe today is the *last* day of tutoring. Time has gone by so fast," Ashley comments, taking more clothes out of the dryer.

"Yeah, Isabella is an excellent student. She did well."

"I'm sure having a fantastic teacher helps too."

I shrug, thinking I can't take the credit for that. "I'm not so sure about that."

Ashley turns to face me. "Isabella adores you. She talks about you all the time."

That's so endearing and sweet of her. "Aw, really? That's so sweet."

"She says that none of Caiden's friends have ever paid attention to her, except for you. She is so happy to have you as her friend."

I'm shocked; that is such an honor.

I'm the lucky one that Isabella even considers *me* her friend.

"No, the pleasure is all mine. I'm happy that she sees me as one."

We continue to pull the rest of the clothes out of the dryer so they can be dusted, sorted, and folded. Ashley comes across a wool burgundy sweater. Almost instinctively, she touches the ring attached to the chain around her neck. Her blue eyes flickered to the locked door across from the laundry room.

For the briefest moment, a hint of sadness flickers in her eyes; then it's immediately replaced with a broad smile before she excuses herself. "I'm going to go take the dishes out of the dishwasher. I'll be right back." Ashley turns to walk away.

As I help her fold the sweaters, I start to wonder what happened to cause such a dark cloud to loom over her.

And that's when it hits me.

How could I have not realized it sooner?

The necklace around her neck looks like a wedding ring. The only reason a person would wear a wedding ring around their neck instead of on their hand is if their spouse had... died.

Ashley's husband, Caiden, and Isabella's father must have... died.

That explains why no one ever talks about him.

It breaks my heart just thinking about it, so I can only imagine the unbearable pain they would feel, having to go on *living* without him.

. . ⌘ . .

Outside, the birds chirping in the trees are like music to my ears. The nearby pond sparkles against the light of the midday sun.

I'm sitting on the grass, my face turning up into a smile as I begin to take in different things about Caiden. The loving way he looks out for his sister (walking on the outside of the sidewalk so that he can protect her), how he is such a good son to his mother, and unlike most kids, he enjoys spending time with his family.

Caiden is such a goofball who loves to poke fun at me. Even so, he can always make me laugh, even when the person he's laughing at is *me*. Even now, Caiden is chasing Isabella around, jokingly plotting to drop a ladybug on her head.

I've got to get a picture of this.

The look on his face is priceless.

Of course, when I'm trying my best to be inconspicuous, does my phone not spoil my plans. To my horror and dismay, I forgot to turn off the flash.

Oh, snap.

Caiden looks over at me now, an amused smirk on his face. "Did you— "

"No." I shake my head adamantly.

His smile grows even bigger. Oh, how I would love to wipe that annoying smirk off his face. "Yeah, I saw you." Caiden points at my phone.

"You saw nothing. It was Is!" I throw my cell phone at her and run away.

Caiden laughs, running after me. "Wait, come back! Here, I'll even pose for you this time. You can take as many pictures as you like!"

I cover my ears. "I can't hear you!"

. . ⚬ . .

I swing my legs back and forth on the swing as the wind gently blows around us. Although I was the one who suggested we hang out on the swings, Caiden is the one that seems to be at peace here.

I think we should stick around here for a little longer.

"What's the one thing you wish you knew how to do?" Caiden asks, turning in his swing to face me. When I don't answer right away, he patiently waits. He's a good listener.

I feel comfortable around him.

"I wish... I knew how to forget."

He nods. I study him, the honesty in his eyes, the frank openness of his face, and my shoulders relax. "Sometimes I think it'd be easier, you know?" I tug at the loose piece of hair tucked behind my ear. "That it would hurt less that way."

"But then... You'd also forget your fondest memories. If erasing my memory also meant losing the good ones, I'd want to keep them all."

I stared at him for a good ten seconds. "You're one of those '*the glass is half-full*' type of guys, aren't you?" I pause, a teasing smile on my face. "The one who *always* sees the bright side."

"You almost make it sound like that's a *bad* thing."

"Oh, come on. People who see the world as full of sunshine and rainbows disgust me."

Caiden smirks, playing along. "The audacity!"

"I know, right!"

There it is. He hits me with that thousand-watt smile, and I smile back, mirroring his.

· · ᴔᴦᴔ · ·

We have dinner together back at the house since today is the last day of Isabella's tutoring. This also means that I will have no more reason to come back here anymore. The thought makes me feel sad.

Caiden made us Shakshouka, an Arabian dish made up of tomatoes simmered in herbs and spices with eggs cracked on top until the heat cooks them. This dish is served with freshly baked bread.

It smells and looks delicious.

I take a bite of the Shakshouka and instantly screw up my face. I think I just bit right into a ball of pepper seasoning. Normally, I'm okay with spicy food, but this time my eyes start to water.

Ugh, how embarrassing.

I need to get a glass of water so I can pull myself together and stop acting like a fool.

Caiden rushes over to me, thinking I'm choking? Because he is about to do the Heimlich Maneuver, before I manage to croak, "Water."

Caiden freezes. He looks... almost mad. "Are you trying to give me a heart attack? I thought you were really choking."

Isabella comes up beside him, handing me a glass of water. I gulp it down, feeling embarrassing for having overreacted.

"Relax," Isabella says to Caiden, sitting him back down. "Stop being such a worrywart."

· · ✺ · ·

Isabella has the mindset to teach me how to play Uno. She was stunned and just couldn't understand how on earth it would be possible that I hadn't played Uno until now. So, after dinner, as promised, Isabella sits across from me, ready to teach me.

This will be fun.

Isabella goes over the rules fairly quickly, then smiles and says, "Okay, ready?"

No, not ready, no.

It all went in one ear and out the next. But, hey, it's just a game, right? Who cares who wins or loses, anyway?

As we begin playing, I observe that there's something different about Isabella. She looks like she has this fire in her eyes, a look I've never seen on her before. Caiden pulls out his phone, eager to record us. I don't know why until Isabella mercilessly defeats me every time.

Oh, she's good.

Caiden watches as I lose yet another game, all the while trying to hide the look of amusement on his face. The look I send his way lets him know he's failed miserably in trying to be discreet.

Then Caiden just loses it. "She beat you... not once... not twice... but six times—in a row!" He rolls over on the ground, laughing so hard I hope he chokes on his spit.

"Thank you. You are a good sport." Isabella extends her hand to me, and I shake it.

I have to admit, that girl's got spunk.

I like it.

"Is, be honest," Caiden says, "you totally asked Athena to play *just so* you could enjoy beating her."

Isabella denies it, but the slight smirk on her face says otherwise.

The time continues to fly, and before I know it, it's already dark outside. It's about time for me to go home.

I'm not ready to say goodbye yet.

"Do you really have to go? Can't you stay a little bit longer?"

"I really wish I could. I'm sorry, Is." I pull her into a hug, gently combing my fingers through her wavy brown hair.

I'm really going to miss her.

Isabella pulls back, placing a gift in my hands. It's a small black velvet photo album. This is so kind of her, and I'm struggling not to cry. "Is, you didn't have to get me anything."

"But I wanted to. I'm really going to miss you."

Oh boy, here comes the waterworks.

Stop it; I'm not causing a scene. "You're going to make me cry."

I glance over at Caiden, sniffling by the door. "Are you... crying?" I turn around to face him.

"No..." He laughs like that's the most ridiculous thing he has ever heard. "There is... something in my eye."

I look over at the two of their sad faces and open my arms wide. "Come here, you guys."

. . ⌘ . .

When I arrive home, I open the photo album from Isabella. She had slipped a note inside it:

"Dear Athena, you have been my best friend. No one ever treated me this way like how you treat me and don't care about my age. People other than you care about my age. If they see I am younger, they won't include me. But you included me in everything, so I want to give you a token of my appreciation." - From Isabella

Now, I'm crying.

I'm crying tears of joy, thinking, what did I do to deserve her?

CHAPTER 13
Athena:

I'M JUST HOPPING OUT of the shower, slipping my toes into my fuzzy pink bath slippers, when I start to feel a little nostalgic. Around this time, I am usually at the Alshaaers' house. It feels weird to be at home when, for so long, I got used to that routine.

Now, it feels weird not to be there anymore.

I grab my diffuser from the bathroom drawer and sit on my bed wrapped up in a towel while I take the time to blow dry my hair carefully. I went for a swim this morning, but I didn't wear my swim cap, so my hair was in knots after. I finished almost half a bottle of conditioner trying to detangle it. I run my fingers through it now, and it is finally tangle-free.

An incoming message pops up on my phone screen. It's from Caiden.

Caiden: What are you doing?
Athena: Nothing, really. Why?
Caiden: Want to come with me to the grocery store? I need help picking out the good fruit.

Athena: Sure.

• • ⟨⟩ • •

I hop in the car heading over to the 'Squeezed Fresh Grocery.' It doesn't take me long to get there. The shop is only fifteen minutes or so from my house.

When I arrive, Caiden is waiting for me in front of the store entrance, waving at me. "Fancy meeting you here. Come here often?" he says, obviously thinking his joke was funny.

"Why are we even still friends?"

"Because I'm awesome, *obviously*."

"That's debatable," I say, grabbing a shopping cart as we walk side by side into the grocery store.

I find a sense of comfort in small towns; everyone has a special way of making you feel at home.

Angela, a red-haired lady with a bright smile, greets us. Angela always smells like apples and brown sugar. She used to babysit us when we were little kids. "Hey A! Who's this?"

"Hi, I'm Caiden. It's nice to meet you." Caiden shakes Angela's hand.

Angela wiggles her eyebrows at me as a mischievous grin spreads across her face. I know exactly what she's thinking before she says it. "Oh my. Sugar, your boyfriend is *very* handsome."

Oh, just perfect. By lunchtime, the word will be spread. The whole neighborhood will think that 'A's got a boyfriend.'

"He's not my—"

"Thank you." Caiden flashes her a smile.

Ugh, great! Another thing for him to tease me about relentlessly.

As soon as we are out of Angela's sight, my eyes dart across the crowded store, looking for somewhere to hide. Ducking behind Caiden, I tell him, "Maybe we shouldn't go grocery shopping together anymore."

"Why not? Don't you like hanging out with me?"

"I do, but—" I stop short when I see more people staring at us and pointing. Rumors spread like wildfire. Word sure got around fast.

I hide around the corner, motioning for him to follow. Caiden slides in beside me, leaning on the shampoo display behind us. "It's giving off the impression that we..." I gesture between us.

"That we're dating?"

"Exactly." I'm glad that he's getting the point, so there is no need for me to have to explain myself.

"Which we're not," Caiden says.

"That's correct."

See?

We are on the same page here. So, there is no need to make this weird or awkward since we agree.

"So then"—he steps closer—"why *don't* we?"

Caiden studies me, making me even more embarrassed and uncomfortable in the process. "You're cute when you're embarrassed," he says with a cheeky smile.

I push past him, but unfortunately, I don't make it far before I crash into the nearby fruit cart. All the apples come tumbling down with me, some bursting open when they reach the floor. Caiden bends down to help pick them up as we salvage what's left of them.

． ． ⌘ ． ．

I refuse to say another word to him on the whole ride home, making Caiden chuckle. I know he is laughing at me; the nerve of this guy to embarrass me like that and then dare to laugh.

Why would he even say something like that, anyway?

"Shut up." I glare in his direction, then turn my eyes back to the road. Caiden had walked to the store, and since I drove, I offered him a ride home.

I am starting to regret that decision.

But he only laughs even more at my reaction.

Finally, I pull up to the driveway of his house, putting the car in park. "What? I didn't even say anything." Caiden asks, all innocently, like he isn't aware of what he is doing.

"Don't care. Shut up." I sulk, unbuckling my seatbelt to open the trunk so Caiden can grab his groceries. But of course, since I was in such a hurry to unbuckle it, the belt bounces back, hitting me smack dab in the face.

Ouch.

I rub where the belt hits me beside the corner of my eye.

"Are you okay?" Caiden reaches over to inspect my face for signs of swelling.

I slap his hands away. "I'm fine."

CHAPTER 14
Caiden:

I'M SITTING ON THE couch, watching the news with Mom, when there is a report of an 11-year-old girl who was kidnapped, and the suspect has yet to be found. The girl has been missing for three days now. Police are asking if anyone has a lead to who it might be or hears of her whereabouts to call 911.

She is only 11 years old.

The same age as Isabella.

I can't even imagine the pain her family is going through right now, that poor little girl. As much as I would love to be by Isabella's side for 24 hours every day, attached at the hip, I know it's impossible. There will be times that Isabella will be on her own, like at school. This kidnapper probably stalked the little girl to and from school, waiting for an opportunity to kidnap her. What kind of sick human being does things like that?

Just the thought of something happening to Isabella *terrifies* me.

I can't let that happen.

Okay, I have an idea. Maybe I can teach Isabella a few self-defense moves. Just in case she ever needs to use them. At least then I would feel at peace knowing that she could protect herself. I hope that day will never come, though.

I pray it doesn't.

• • ∞ • •

"I'm not always going to be around to protect you." I adjust the straps on Isabella's gloves, securing them around her wrists. "You're going to have to learn how to protect yourself."

We have only been practicing for about 20 minutes when Isabella throws her gloves on the floor.

"I'm done. This is too hard," she says, frustrated.

"Come on, Isabella. I know you can do this. Keep trying," I plead with her, picking the gloves up from the floor. "No, we are not done. I am not leaving until you learn how to do it."

"I'm tired." Isabella tries to walk off, but I grab her arm.

"Show me the flip."

Stomping her feet, Isabella whines. "Caiden-"

"Now!"

Isabella tries it again but doesn't use enough force to pick me up off the ground. "Again."

Isabella does it again, this time having more control by bending her legs. "Better, but not good enough.

Again."

Irritated by my demands, Isabella, nonetheless, makes another attempt.

"C'mon, put your back into it!"

That was the last straw—something inside Isabella snaps.

She takes me out with a single blow.

Huffing and puffing, Isabella throws her gloves at me. "You're such a jerk!" She storms off, leaving me lying on the floor. My arm is sore from smacking the hardwood on the floor.

Aw man, Isabella must be furious at me.

I need to go apologize. I shouldn't have yelled at her like that; it wasn't called for.

I knock on her bedroom door to see if she's okay. Isabella had left the door open just a crack; she's curled up in her bed, crying.

Slowly, I open her bedroom door. "Is..." I call out, feeling guilty for making her cry. "I'm... I'm sorry."

Pulling down the covers revealed her tear-stricken face. "So, you're—you're going to leave me too?"

I'm at a loss for words.

"No... Is... of course not."

"If that's your plan..."—Isabella sniffles—"leave... just go now. I don't want to see you anymore!"

I kneel by her bed, shaking my head. "Is, I—"

"Don't. Just leave." Isabella's tone is cold; hostile.

I pick up a chair from the side of her room, plop it down in front of her bed, and state firmly, "No. I'm not going anywhere." I hold my ground and refuse to leave until she falls asleep.

Soon she's sleeping soundly, so I put the chair back at her desk, turning towards the door to leave.

Isabella's eyes fly open. "Please... please don't leave me."

I cradle her in my arms, promising her, "You can't get rid of me that easily. I'm here, and as long as you need me to be, I'll *always* be here."

I sing to her until she falls back to sleep, snoring peacefully, but I can't bring myself to sleep. I am in a trance, haunted by the words replaying in my mind.

On the night, our lives were changed forever.

I start to feel hot and stuffy, so I step outside into the cool, crisp night air. Breathing in the cold air, my breath comes out like a cloud of smoke as I break into a run.

•• ൡ ••

My lungs are filled with thick layers of smoke and gasoline.

Gasping for air, I try to breathe. Hot crimson-coloured blood is seeping through into the fabric of the car seats. My head rings and swells from the glass blades stuck to the sides of my face.

"Dad?" My eyes try to refocus in the darkness. Prying open the passenger door, I half drag my body across the scalding hot asphalt.

I walk for what feels like an eternity but stop dead in my tracks when I see a limp figure over the hill ahead of me.

My heart drops.

My body screams from the pain, but I fight it, although it takes every ounce of energy I have left to move.

I dash down the hill. "Dad!" I cry out but hear no answer.

Kneeling, I try my best to shake Dad awake. "Dad, wake up! Help is on the way, please... please..." My Dad's body lays there still as a stone.

Leaning over, I put a finger under his nose, but he's not breathing.

I rest my head on his chest. What I do not hear sends me into a panic.

"Please!!" I clutch my chest, pleading. "I'm sorry." Tears spring from my eyes. "I was wrong... It's all my fault! Please..." I beg. "Please don't leave me."

· · ✧ · ·

Early the next morning, I'm startled when the doorbell rings. Isabella is fast asleep, so I rush to get it, so the noise doesn't wake her.

I'm surprised to see that it's Sky at the door. "Hey, Sky, what brings you by?"

Sky holds up her hands, full of baking supplies. "Isabella and I are making cupcakes today; we have to make 100 for the bake sale tomorrow."

Oh man, that was today, wasn't it?

"Oh, I'm sorry, Sky. Isabella's... not feeling well today."

"Is she okay?"

"Uh, yeah. Yeah, she will be."

"Okay. I guess I'll go then." Sky's shoulders slump a little as she walks away.

I feel bad. After all, it's my fault Isabella stayed up all night. "Hey, Sky? How about I help you make the cupcakes?"

Sky turns to look at me. "Really?"

"Yes, really."

"That would be wonderful, thank you."

I open the door wider. "Come on in."

· · ᴏᴸᴏ · ·

Sky has a knack for picking up things pretty quickly. She is skilled at cracking eggs and decorating cupcakes. Sky takes her time with it to make sure that each cupcake is covered with the right amount of icing.

I try to make conversation while we work, but Sky silences me. "Shh..." She puts a finger to her lips, telling me to zip it.

So instead, I watch her at work, admiring her skill and dedication.

After a while, Sky stretches her neck. She looks tired. We have been going at this for a while and have made fifty cupcakes so far. I could always finish them for her.

"Do you need a break? I can take over—"

"No, I need you to leave."

"What?"

"Your presence is giving me a headache." Sky rubs her temples, making me chuckle.

Clearly, I am encroaching on her workspace, and she wants to work solo.

"Alright, alright. I'll leave you to it then."

· · ᴏᴸᴏ · ·

I sit on the front porch watching the fluffy white clouds drift across the clear blue sky. Mom walks up to me with grocery bags in her hands. "Caiden, what are you doing out here?"

I take the grocery from her. "I've been kicked out."

Mom shakes her head, smiling as she walks inside. "Oh, what a pleasant surprise." Mom coos when she sees Sky and Isabella hard at work decorating the cupcakes.

So it *wasn't* that Sky wanted to work alone; she just didn't want to work with... me. "So, Is can be in the kitchen with you, but not *me*."

"What?" Mom asks, but I wave it off.

"It's nothing. I'm just not wanted. It's fine."

"Speak clearly and stop mumbling," Mom says.

. . ✒ . .

I roll over on my bed in my room, wondering what I did wrong. Luna climbs onto the bed with me.

"You like having me around, right?" Luna licks me on the cheek. I will take that as a yes.

Smiling, I am elated when I see a text from Athena.

Athena: What was the best phase in your life or your fondest memory?

I think back to the time that I felt the most carefree and full of life, back when Dad was alive.

Caiden: When I was ten years old because I miss the days when I was young and fearless.

Athena: Let's do something childish. Like back in the hot summer elementary school days when we used to have relay races: Guys vs. Girls.

Caiden: You should be prepared to lose.

Athena: Never underestimate me. Name the time and place; you're on.

We agree to bring all the family together next Saturday to do a relay race.

This should be entertaining.

CHAPTER 15

Athena:

"NO ONE EVER COMPLIMENTS me!" Rain complains, smacking down her artwork on the kitchen table.

Sky gives her a look. "Oh, so you need compliments to complete you?"

Alex shakes his head. "You poor, pitiful child. Come here." He opens his arms wide; Rain shoves his hands away.

"Don't touch me," Rain says.

"I'm serious. You guys really need your own TV show," Violet says, taking a break from cutting up the watermelon. "People would love you."

"Of course they would. Have you seen this face?" Alex smiles creepily.

I cough into my sleeve. "Delusional." Alex throws a fry at my head. Surprisingly, he has pretty good aim but still misses his target because I duck.

"Enough," Mom warns.

Ah, that's right. I should double-check the address before we end up at the wrong place.

Athena: Can you text me the address for the park, please?
Caiden: Looking for an excuse to text me, I see.

I roll my eyes, thinking *someone* thinks too highly of himself.

Athena: Don't flatter yourself.
Caiden: I'm just playing.
Athena: Hmm

I must have had a strange look on my face because when I look up from my phone, I find five pairs of eyes staring back at me. "Take a picture; it'll last longer," I say, just as Rain snaps a photo of me.

"Another one to add to my collection of 'Athena's most embarrassing moments,'" Rain says, spreading her hands out.

If Rain dares to do something crazy, like blowing it up on a poster, she's a dead woman walking.

I charge at Rain, lunging for her phone. "Delete it, you creep."

Alex just sits there like a lump on a log, as usual, clearly enjoying the show. "This family is hysterical.

Who knows, maybe one day someone might just write about us in a book," Alex says.

Caiden:

ONCE EVERYTHING IS all set up and everyone is organized into teams, the team captains just need to give the signal and...

"A! V!" A tall black man dressed in a dark blue shirt wraps Athena up in a bear hug. Giggling, she hugs him back.

Umm... who is he?

And why does he have his arms around her?

Violet runs up to join the hug. "Move over. I want a hug too!"

"Ah, two of my favorite girls fighting over me." The tall man grins. "It doesn't get better than this."

"Stop it, you two. You need to learn how to share," Mom says, walking over to the three of them.

"Well, hello, Josiah."

"Well, if it isn't the most beautiful woman I've ever laid my eyes on," Josiah says.

"Oh, you charmer." Nicola places her hands on both of his cheeks to take a good look at him. "You get more and more handsome every time I see you. That said, it'd be nicer if I got to *see* you more often."

Josiah hangs his head. "I know. I'm sorry. As a peace offering, I've come bearing gifts."

"Me first!" Sky prances over.

Josiah crouches down to meet Sky at her level. "Excuse me, young lady. I'm looking for a little girl; her name is Sky. Have you seen her?"

Sky laughs. "It's me, silly! Sky!" She twirls around. "See?"

"No way! I barely recognize you. You've grown up into such a beautiful young lady."

"Why, thank you, good sir." Sky does a little curtsey.

"Hey, man." Alex strolls over.

Josiah turns around with a look of shock on his face. "Am I the only one that heard that?"

"Heard what?" Violet asks.

"The sound of a *grown* man." Josiah claps Alex on the back. "Gosh, man, time sure does fly. How've you been, man?"

"Can't you tell? I'm doing great."

Athena rolls her eyes. "Yup and his personality sure stayed the same, unfortunately." Alex leans over, smacking her on the back of the head.

"Hey now, be a good brother, and don't beat up your sister. A woman this lovely, you should cherish her." Josiah winks at her.

"Hear that? I'm lovely."

"Clearly, he's gone deaf *and* blind since we last saw him," Alex grumbles.

Josiah pinches Athena's cheeks, telling her how pretty she's become while he's been away.

Alright, enough is enough.

At that, I clap my hands a little too enthusiastically, startling everyone by shouting through the megaphone.

"Alright, everybody, let's get this show on the road!"

I smile when Athena and Josiah pull apart, covering their ears to block out the loud sound.

Mission accomplished.

• • ⌘ • •

Everyone is all lined up and ready to go for the 3-legged race. Isabella & Sky, Violet & Rain, Alex & I, and last but not least...

Athena & Josiah.

Collin blows the whistle to signal that the race has begun, just as Josiah stops Collin for some reason.

"Wait one second." Josiah places a hand on Athena's shoulder to stop her, bending down to tie her untied shoelaces.

Athena smiles sweetly at him, patting Josiah's head adoringly. "You're the sweetest."

Josiah smiles up at her. "I know."

I chug down my water, then crumple up the bottle before hurling it in the nearby trash bin.

Alex walks over to me. "Dude, what's wrong with you?"

"Nothing. Nothing." I shuffle my feet back and forth, trying to ignore how insecure I'm feeling.

• • ⚬∞ • •

Later, after everyone is sitting down to eat, I shuffle around the food on my plate, a permanent scowl on my face. I don't even care that I'm pouting like a two-year-old who is mad that Mom says no sweets.

And he loves sweets.

Isabella pokes me in the stomach. "Hey, why the long face?"

When I don't reply, she looks over my shoulder to see what I'm staring at.

I'm blatantly staring at Athena and Josiah, who are at the picnic table directly across from us.

"You're such a slob," Josiah tells Athena as she throws a fry at him. "The food is supposed to go in your *mouth,* not everywhere else."

"Shut up."

"Ew, gross, you spit on my face!" Josiah squirms as Athena tries to wipe it off.

Isabella turns her attention back to me. "Oh, I see why you're sulking now."

"What?"

Isabella stares at me for a few seconds without saying anything.

"You see what?"

"You are jealous." Isabella smiles. "It's written all over your face."

"Jealous?"

Isabella nods, taking a sip from her Sprite.

"That's ridiculous," I scoff like that's the craziest thing I have ever heard because that *is* the craziest thing I've ever heard. Why in the world would I be—

"*Is it?*" Isabella says in a sing-song voice that I don't like very much.

I clear my throat. "Stop talking nonsense."

She shrugs as if to say she's given up on me.

I stack our paper plates and cups, cleaning up all the garbage.

Beside me, Isabella and Sky are having a water gunfight. My eyes land on the water gun in Isabella's hands.

"Hey, give me that for a second." A mischievous grin spreads across my face as I snatch the gun from Isabella, setting my aim on my target.

Isabella tries to snatch it back from me. "Hey—"

Without hesitation, I point the water gun toward Josiah, completely soaking him.

Isabella shoots me an "I told you so" look, shaking her head at my childish behavior.

Okay, so maybe I am jealous.

Just a teeny-bit.

CHAPTER 16

Caiden:

ALEX INVITED ME OVER to his place to watch the Raptor's Championship game. He told me not to bring anything, but I didn't feel right showing up empty-handed. My Mom raised me better than that. So, I picked up a few things at the store to bring with me. I also found this cool basketball mug that I thought Alex would like.

I ring the doorbell, and Alex opens the door. "What's all this?" he says, gesturing to the two full bags of snacks in my hands.

"Oh, nothing, just some snacks and drinks."

"I told you I would have some."

Stepping inside, I toss him the mug. "It's a gift." Alex gives me a look. "I heard if you want someone to like you, you should give them a gift."

"Uh-huh." Alex heads into the kitchen to get bowls for the chips.

As I sit down on the couch, Alex cocks his head at me. "*Why* exactly do you want me to like you?"

I feel a bit uneasy as Alex continues to stare at me like he's trying to bore holes into my skull with his eyes.

"Because we are friends." I laugh and add, "Friends should like each other."

"Who says we were friends?"

I scratch the back of my head. Okay, *maybe* saying that we were friends right off the bat wasn't the best idea. It came off a little too strong.

Alex sits down on the couch, and we watch the game. "So... were you always a basketball fan?" I ask in a lame attempt to make conversation.

"Yeah. Ever since my d—" Alex cuts himself off without finishing the sentence, his eyes fixed on the TV screen.

I don't ask him to repeat what he was going to say.

The Raptors are in the lead 13-11. I'm on the edge of my seat as they make another score.

Yes!

I look to Alex, who still seems... off... distracted. "Is everything alright?" I press pause on the TV.

Alex seems to almost snap out of it for a second. "Hey yeah... I'm good." Alex says although it doesn't seem like he means it.

I decided that maybe I should shut up and not say anything else.

The silence stretches on for a while with just the sound of the basketballs bouncing off the floor.

Alex sighs. "My uh... my Dad taught me everything I know about basketball and boxing. When he took me boxing, he'd drill it into me that I should fight for what I want and never let it go." Alex smiles like he's amused, but he looks the complete opposite. "Which is ironic because that's *exactly* the opposite of what he chose to do."

That must have been terrible.

"That sucks, man. I'm sorry."

Alex shakes his head. "It's whatever." He gets up to grab a drink from the kitchen like he wants to drop the subject.

That's fine. I don't want to push him to talk about it.

"Hey uh..." I call Alex from the couch. "Is Josiah..."

Let's just rip it off like a band-aid. "You know, related to you guys?"

Without missing a beat, Alex says, "He's practically a part of the family."

"So, he's... he's not blood-related or anything like that?"

Alex closes the fridge door. "Why?" I can feel the defensiveness in his tone of voice.

"Oh uh... no reason. It was a random question. Do I have to have a reason?"

Alex walks back to the couch, studying me for a bit.

"Just curious, that's all," I say, pressing play on the TV.

"Uh-huh."

I straighten in my seat. "Yeah."

Alex drinks some of his Pepsi. "Okay."

CHAPTER 17

Athena:

I SNUGGLE UP UNDER the covers, delighted to finally get the chance to curl up in my bed and enjoy reading again. Reading is one of the few times I feel completely at peace. I am free from inconvenient thoughts and feelings in a world other than my own.

Feelings are overrated.

Moments later, feeling hot and stuffy, I crack open my window to let in some air. That's when I notice the car parked outside our house. Sitting up to take a closer look, I start to see that it's a car I've seen before.

Okay, let's not jump to conclusions.

Out of the 3.7 billion people that live on this planet, there is a pretty good chance that *thousands* of people have the same car. Shaking the thought from my mind, I tell myself that I'm just seeing things.

Clearly, I am exhausted and need to get some sleep.

The following morning, I wake up feeling well-rested and refreshed. It's beautiful weather outside today. The birds are chirping outside my bedroom window. I practically skip outside, still in my pajamas, humming along to the song in my head.

As I open the lid to the garbage bin to throw out the trash, something catches the corner of my eye. Dropping the bag to the floor, I now know my eyes are not fooling me anymore.

Standing on the edge of the sidewalk is the man I swore I would never lay my eyes on again.

Until I did.

What—

What is *Dad* doing here?

I stare at him in shock, unable to believe this is really happening. Dad takes a step toward me. "I should have told you the truth. I know I should have told you, but I didn't want... to devastate you. I knew that... I would lose you, and I—I just couldn't lose you."

It feels like my brain has short-circuited. Even though I can see him and I can hear his voice, my mind isn't able to process what is going on. It is too surreal.

Dad pauses to clear his throat. "I never... I should never have broken my little girl's heart. I'm sorry that I'm a failure as a father."

The part that I can't seem to wrap my head around is, why *now*?

Why come back into our lives now, not ten or even fifteen years ago?

A volcano of emotions that I held in for years come pouring out. "Do you know how long... how long... I waited for you?" I ask but don't wait for him to answer. "I waited for you every single day for six *years*, but you *never* showed up." I meet his gaze. "You weren't there when I needed you."

I didn't have a choice back then, so I'm making it now.

"So, don't bother to show up now. As you can see, I'm all grown up. In fact, I'm doing just *great* without you." I silence the cry rising in my throat. "I don't need you anymore. So just go—go away."

Dad opens his arms to hug me, but I shrug him off. "Don't, just don't."

I start walking away as Dad reaches out to stop me. His lips are moving, but I can't hear a word he's saying. My mind is fuzzy, and all I want is to go back inside.

Alex slips in between us, keeping me behind him. "You know what, why don't *you* just leave?" Smirking, he adds, "You're great at that."

Dad looks at us as if he is about to say something, then obediently does as he is told, leaving Alex and me standing on the driveway.

• • ∽ • •

I follow Alex back inside the house. Flinging open the cupboard door, Alex rummages around for some snacks. "How can someone be so shamelessly selfish?" he asks, annoyed, ripping open a bag of chips with his teeth. "What kind of man just gets up and abandons his responsibilities like that?"

I look at Alex, wondering how he can be so insanely chill about all this.

Yeah, he's upset, but I feel like he is taking it really well, considering that the man he used to call Dad just showed up 13 *years* after abandoning him with not even *one* phone call or letter of explanation. So, yes, I'm amazed that he can remain so incredibly calm.

"I don't know. Up until now, it still doesn't make sense. Yet here we are, letting this bother us. How unfair is it that we are sitting here in anger while he gets to just... disappear?" Snatching the bag of chips from him, I grab a handful.

"It's actually kind of funny."

Alex is the only one that can fully understand.

Alex & I are Dad's biological children. Rain and Sky are Collin's kids that he had before he married Mom. We are all like real siblings now, but when it comes to this, I'm glad I have someone that is on my side.

At least there is one person who knows how I feel.

• • ∽ • •

Heading upstairs to my bedroom, I pull open the wooden drawer of my nightstand where I have an old art kit. It has been almost a decade since

I last took a crack at it. I remember when it was my favourite thing in the world.

I collect the array of paint colors and markers, bringing all the supplies to the paint easel tucked away in the corner of my room. As I pull off the thick grey cover, clouds of dust fill the air. Tossing it aside, I lift the paintbrush and begin to paint.

With no clear direction or intention in mind, I simply paint what I am feeling. Rage flowing through me like lava; one more push and I will overflow. The paint splatters everywhere as I continue to add thicker layers of red, black, orange, and yellow. What started as a calming art project has turned into an atrocious catastrophe.

Having had enough, I tread to the bathroom to take a much-needed shower. I'm scrubbing away at the paint speckles that cover my arms and legs, but the paint refuses to come off. "Why won't it just go away?"

I scrub harder and harder until my skin is raw. At this rate, I won't be able to stop until it bleeds.

. . ⌘ . .

Turning on the shower, I let the hot water wash over me—puddles of multicoloured paint pool at my feet. I'm surprisingly numb to the heat, although by now, it should start to burn. Clutching the pipe head, I turn it off, needing a moment to breathe.

My throat closes, and my head swells as the heat sucks all the air out of me.

Sliding onto the shower floor, I cradle my arms around myself to still the shaking. "It's okay, Athena." I pat myself on the shoulder. "It's going to be..." I take in a sharp breath. "Okay."

"Don't worry; you'll be fine." My voice trembles as I struggle to keep my composure.

"You're fine. You're okay. You're..." My breathing is unsteady. "You're going... you're going to be okay."

CHAPTER 18

Athena:

CAIDEN BURSTS THROUGH the salon doors, saying he desperately needs a haircut. His brown curly hair flops into his eyes. Blowing back the loose curls, he gives me a once over.

I excuse myself, saying I will be right back to April, who is standing by the front desk. Moving to wash my hands, I dry them on the towel hanging at the edge of the sink. "Please don't just openly stare at me like that," I say.

"Like what?"

"You know what I mean. Just don't—don't look at me at all. I'm working, and you're kind of distracting me."

"Oh, really?" Caiden says, with a smirk on his face.

Glancing over Caiden's shoulder, I can see April watching us.

"Cut it out." With that, I tighten my apron and proceed to clean up my styling tools. I finished with my last customer for the day, so now I can head home.

"Wait, why are you packing up? You haven't cut my hair yet," Caiden whines.

"Sorry, shop's closed. Time to go home."

"Well, I guess I'm just going to have to stay here until you change your mind." Caiden plops down on the salon chair, spinning around like a kid on a teacup ride at the amusement park.

I chide him for being so childish. "Oh, how *mature*."

I slowly pick up my hair scissors that are on the counter in front of him, which immediately freaks him out.

"Hold on a second." Caiden darts his eyes around like he is terrified. "Don't do something you're going to regret."

"I have no idea what you're talking about," I say with the scissors still hovering over his head. Catching a glimpse of the worried look on his face in the mirror, I laugh.

Messing with him is fun.

• • ✑ • •

Whipping out my black silk cape from under the counter, I wrap it around his shoulders. "So, what haircut did you have in mind?"

Caiden doesn't even ponder about it for a moment. "Surprise me."

"Fearless, aren't we? You trust me that much?"

"I trust you completely."

"Well, you probably shouldn't."

I spritz his hair with water and start combing through the curls with my fingers, taking a few silver clips to separate his hair into sections first. I lightly dust off the ends of his hair, shaping it as I go along.

When I make it to the front of his hair, I ensure to cut it very carefully.

Okay, I think it looks pretty good. "Take a look," I say, satisfied with my work.

Actually, now that I'm looking at the bangs again, I need to trim just one more section.

Caiden opens his eyes just as I'm about to go back in to make one more minor adjustment to the front. "It's perfect," he says without looking at it. His eyes are fixed on me.

Breaking the stare, I lean down to unwrap the cape around his neck. "Well, lucky for you, I didn't get too scissor-happy, so you still have hair left."

"And I'm very grateful for that." Caiden gets up from his chair, moving over to where April is at the front desk so that he can pay.

"That'll be twelve dollars," I say. He hands me a twenty-dollar bill, and I give him his change.

"Isabella misses her tutor," Caiden blurts out, not quite meeting my eyes.

Well, that was random.

Especially since Isabella and I talk quite frequently, we text each other pretty much every other day. "Oh, does she?"

"Yeah, but she's too shy to tell you that," Caiden rambles like he is nervous or something.

This is entertaining.

"Oh, really?"

"Yeah, so I thought I'd do it for her."

"How very kind of you," I say, trying to hide the smile playing on my lips. "Thank you."

It's endearing, really, the way he is acting all nervous and jittery.

"Well..." I wiggle my eyebrows at him. "You can let Isabella know she is *more* than welcome to call or text me when she misses me."

"I sure will," Caiden says, but realizing his mistake, quickly back-tracks. "I mean, I sure will. I'll be sure to do that... I mean, tell her that." My eyes crinkle at the corners, beaming up at him.

. . ⚘ . .

When Caiden leaves, I grab the broom to start sweeping. "Who's that?" April pops up behind me out of nowhere, startling me.

"Geesh, April, could you make a sound and not sneak up on me like that?"

"Don't change the subject." April raises a blonde eyebrow. "You didn't tell me you had a *boyfriend*."

I laugh. "Uh, yeah, because I don't. We are just *friends*."

April makes a noise at the back of her throat. "What?" I ask, knowing full well that I'm not going to like what she has to say.

April only does that when she knows that she is right about something.

"Oh, nothing," April says while she counts the money in the cash register.

I sigh. "Just say it." I mean, she is going to end up telling me eventually, anyway. April just likes to have me begging on my knees, wanting to know what she will say.

"It's just that... friends don't look at each other that way," April says.

We are *just* friends, though.

Aren't we?

. . ⚬∾ . .

Later that evening, Josiah comes over to our place for dinner. Mom is so ecstatic to see him, and I bet you any money that if she were left to her own devices, she would have already adopted Josiah if she could.

Never mind the fact that he *already* has two parents that love him.

Mom always treats Josiah like royalty whenever he is around. Exhibit A. "Here," Mom says, passing the *best* pieces of the Maple Glazed chicken in front of us to Josiah's plate. "Have some more."

I look down at my plate, which has only one sad little piece of chicken on it. Josiah takes a piece of chicken from his plate, placing it on mine. Aw, someone cares about me after all.

"Psst... Psst." Alex is standing by the kitchen doorway, waving at me frantically.

Man, I am so hungry. All I want to do is eat. What is he going on about over there?

I sigh. 'What?' I mouth to him, annoyed that he is taking precious time away from my dinner. Alex just keeps waving me over. Reluctantly I get up from my seat, thinking that he better make it quick or else.

"What do you want?" I say, now standing in front of him.

"So..." Alex wiggles his eyebrows.

I have no time for his foolishness. Alex needs to get to the point already. "You're acting weirder than normal. What's wrong with you?"

"What do you think of J?"

I wrinkle my brows, confused by the question. "What do you mean, what do I *think*? What is there to think about?"

"Oh, come on, stop being so dense. You guys would be great together."

I practically fall over laughing. In fact, I laugh so hard that I almost choke on my spit. "That's a good one. You really had me for a second there."

But Alex isn't laughing. "You can't be serious," I say.

"Hear me out here, okay? Who *else* is going to be willing to put up with you and all of your..." He gestures up and down. "Personality."

I give him a warning stare. "I'm not liking where this conversation is going."

Alex holds his hands out in front of him. "All I'm asking is for you to *consider* it. Josiah's a great guy."

All I can think is that Alex has completely lost it.

Too many hits in the head while boxing; that must be it.

We go back to the dinner table, where I take my seat beside Josiah. Finally, I can eat. I am beyond hungry. Yes! The food is still warm. Digging in, I glance up to see Alex wink at me; I ignore him, refusing to acknowledge his existence.

Alex puts down his fork, having already inhaled his plate of food. "So, J... what do you think of Athena? You know, as a *woman*?"

This time I really start choking.

Josiah pats my back, handing me a glass of water. What just happened? Did Alex actually say that... Please tell me this is not happening right now.

Collin and Mom glance at each other, smiling.

About what I don't know because this is not a smiling matter. This is...

Rain, as usual, pulls out her phone, documenting the whole thing only to add to the embarrassment. Perfect, she might as well document this humiliating experience. Why not?

"Athena, can I talk to you for a second?" Josiah's voice sounds different, almost nervous, which is unlike him.

Alex pushes me out of my seat. "Yes, go ahead." He grins. "You can have her; you have my blessing."

I glare at him. If looks could kill, Alex would be dead.

. . ⌘ . .

We walk up the carpeted stairway leading to my bedroom. For some reason, I'm feeling wary about it. I'm not sure if I want to sit on the bed or the chair. Suddenly more aware of the fact that we are in my *bedroom*—even though Josiah has been in my room countless times before.

I hesitantly glance in his direction, wondering if he took what Alex said to heart. But at the same time, Josiah has known Alex for years, so he would know better than to take Alex too seriously, right?

"Do you... see me as a woman?" I asked him.

Josiah moves closer to me on the bed. In a low voice, he answers with, "Why? Do you see me as a man?"

Every single second that passes by feels like torture, with me unable to answer him.

Josiah throws a pillow at my head, laughing. "You dork. Of course I do, but that doesn't mean I want to *date* you."

Suddenly I'm offended. "But why? Why don't you want to date me?"

He's still laughing at me. Figures. But then, Josiah's face goes back to serious when he mentions that he heard about my dad.

My guess is Alex or Violet must have told him.

"So, what happened?" Josiah asks, wanting my side of the story, but that's just it; there *isn't* one.

"Nothing."

"Athena—" Josiah starts, wanting me to explain further.

"No, really, there's nothing to talk about. He wants to talk, and I just don't want to hear his excuses."

Josiah tilts my chin toward him so he can see the expression on my face. Growing up, that was something that he would do to see if you were telling the truth.

"I'm fine," I say, a response that's become so automatic, almost second nature to me now.

CHAPTER 19
Caiden:

ATHENA INSISTED ON making me dinner since every time she comes over, I always cook. I told her that she didn't have to feel obligated or anything, but she would not take no for an answer.

Athena also told me that she isn't much of a cook, so I think it will be fun to watch her at work.

Athena moves over to the stove, adjusting the temperature to preset it to 360 Degrees Fahrenheit. I pretend to be shocked. "You know how to do that?"

"Shut up."

At this point, I'm purposely trying to get on her nerves; teasing her is so much fun.

I hover over her shoulder, making sure to get her to second guess every decision she makes, like when she pours the salt. "You *sure* you want to do that?"

"Cut it out."

"Okay, okay," I say, promising to leave her alone now.

Though, I didn't really mean it.

Athena reaches for the seasoning in the cupboard. I try to resist the urge to say something, but I just can't help myself. "Are you—"

"One more peep out of you"—Athena narrows her eyes at me—"and I'm going to kill you."

I cackle happily. "Okay fine. I'll be in the living room if you need me."

After Athena is all finished in the kitchen, she comes to join me on the couch while I'm playing fetch with Luna. "Do you smell something burning?" She asks, her nose sniffing the air.

"Is that—"

Athena turns to me. "Didn't you set a timer?"

Wait a second; am I missing something here?

Last I checked, Athena was the one cooking, not me. "I thought you did! That was your job, not mine."

She storms off to the kitchen. "Can't you do anything right? You had *one* job!"

. . ᵒᶠᵒ . .

Athena serves me a plate of what is now burnt Pesto-Stuffed Chicken. It still looks... edible. It just has a certain barbequed feel to it.

I'm about to take the first bite. Athena looks at me expectantly, her eyes wide and hopeful.

"How is it? Be honest."

I chew and swallow, thinking that it's not terrible. Just a little bit overcooked, that's all. "It's got an interesting... flavour. It's... unique."

"It's terrible, isn't it?"

"No, I wouldn't go that far."

She looks genuinely disappointed; I can tell that she wanted it to turn out well.

"Hey, it's okay. You can't be great at *everything;* you have to leave something for the rest of us." I beam, hoping to make her feel better.

It works because Athena is smiling brightly.

"Whatever," Athena says, crossing her legs on the couch. "I have a crazy idea."

I prop my hands under my chin, eager to hear all about it. "Tell me more." I wiggle my eyebrows.

She giggles, the corner of her mouth turning up into a smile. "Ah, never mind." Athena waves her hands in front of her face.

Nope, way too late to back out now.

"What? No, you can't do me dirty like that. Why bring it up then?"

"Let's pretend I didn't say anything." Athena picks up the remote, switching on the TV.

I take the remote from her. "Will it help if I turn around? Will it be less pressure then?" I turn my back to her. "Okay, whenever you are ready. Lay it on me."

"Okay..." Athena sighs. "Umm... Violet and I have always dreamed of having our own dance studio one day. I mean, it was just a silly pipe dream at the time, but I started thinking, what if we did it? We would have to save up for five years or so, but..."

I turn back around, an excited grin on my face. "I know... it's a stupid idea," Athena mutters, looking down at her hands.

I grab her by the shoulders, smiling. "No, it's not stupid at all. You'll do great."

Athena doesn't look too convinced. "I mean... what if I fail?"

"And what if you *don't*?"

"Yeah, well, I don't want to get my hopes up... it'll only lead to disappointment."

"Or..." I shift my legs on the couch, crossing mine too. "Maybe... you'll be pleasantly surprised."

Athena rolls her eyes, but I see the smile on her face. "Forever an optimist."

Luna nudges Athena's knee with the tennis ball in her mouth. She wants to play fetch. Athena throws the ball for her lightly. If she threw it too hard, it would knock down the glass vase on top of the coffee table in the corner.

"Go, get it, girl," Athena tells Luna, who skips off to retrieve it, wagging her tail in excitement.

. . ⌘ . .

The movie Wonder is playing on the TV. Athena is obsessed with this movie. "I can't get over how unbelievable Auggie's parents are. They are hands down the *best* parents ever. I hope to be as good as a parent someday."

They are pretty awesome.

"What about you?" Athena asked me. "Do you want to have kids? You would make a great father."

I'm not so sure about that. I don't even know that I will be...

Never mind, it's best not to think about it.

"I don't know..." I run a hand through my hair. "I'm not sure I'm cut out for that."

"Are you crazy? If anyone would be a good parent, it would be you."

I admire her confidence, but I can't say that I share her enthusiasm.

Luna comes back, tennis ball in her mouth. I take the tennis ball from her, picking her up so she can sit beside us on the couch. "So, Luna, what do you think of Athena?" I whisper in Luna's ear. "Do you like her as much as I do?"

Luna barks, making me chuckle. "So, should we keep her?"

Luna barks again.

"I'm glad you agree." I smooth Luna's soft, milky-white fur. "But between you and me"—I sneak a glance in Athena's direction—"she is a terrible cook. Don't let her go in the kitchen unattended when I'm not here, okay, girl?"

"Hey!" Athena smacks me on the shoulder.

· · ໒‍‍໒ · ·

After the movie ends, Athena gets up, saying that she should probably get going now. "Oh, okay." I try not to sound too disappointed about it, but I am.

I don't want her to leave.

My heart starts to wonder what it would be like if I didn't hold back and tell her how I felt about her.

I solemnly wave goodbye, watching as she drives away.

I head over to the kitchen sink, washing the dishes left over from the dinner Athena made. When I'm finished, I open the bottom cupboard to get Luna's dog food; pouring the brown pebbles into her bowl, I call out for her to come to eat.

Nothing.

Luna isn't coming.

That's odd. Usually, as soon as I *pour* the food out, Luna hears the sound and comes running.

"Luna," I call out, looking for her. "Luna, where are you, girl?" I'm walking up the stairs, wondering where she went. When Luna is too quiet, it usually means she is up to no good. One time we found her with her entire head stuck in a tub of ice cream. It was the cutest thing ever, but cleaning up after was not so cute.

The linen closet in the hallway is open. Someone must have forgotten to lock it. That was probably me when I went to put away the sheets from the laundry.

Luna pops her head out. "There you are, girl; what are you doing in there?" Luna barks, brushing her nose against the cylinder-shaped black bag lying in the corner on the floor.

I was so excited to get this telescope.

As a kid, I was obsessed with the moon and the stars. The vast number of stars, galaxies, and planets in outer space intrigued me. It was mind-blowing. I remember saving up all the money I ever had from lunch money, allowances, lemonade stands, car washes, you name it. I was determined to have enough money to buy a telescope. Dad was so impressed that I was working so hard to save money that he offered to chip in. I only managed to save up around 150 dollars, and Dad worked overtime at the hospital just so that he could pay for the rest.

Dad and I planned to drive down north, a few hours away, to see the Lunar Eclipse. I was ecstatic. I marked each day leading up to it down on my calendar. I couldn't wait to go.

It was going to be our very first father and son bonding trip.

. . ✧ . .

When the day arrived for us to leave, I started getting a little antsy when Dad didn't make it home in time. Dad called, saying he had been pulled into emergency surgery at the hospital and would be late.

"Don't forget that today is the day we have our father and son trip," I told him over the phone, hoping he didn't change his mind about going.

When Dad arrived home, Mom voiced concern about him driving late at night. By now, it was close to 9 p.m.

"Are you sure tonight is still a good day to go?" Mom asked Dad, putting a hand on the small of his back.

Dad kissed Mom's hand, smiling over at me. "I made a promise, and I intend to keep it. Right, kiddo?"

"Right." I smiled back.

Luna barks, pulling me back from the flashback.

I put the telescope back, closing the door to the linen closet. "I'm sorry, girl, let's get you some food." I follow Luna down the stairs to the kitchen, where she eagerly gobbles down her food.

. . ✧ . .

In bed, I'm wide awake, the noise of the ceiling fan buzzing over my head. My mind takes me back to after the car accident, the day that he... Even now, I can barely bring myself to say the words out loud. Out of the fear that if I said it, it would make it real, that Dad would be gone forever.

After the shock, the realization hits like a punch in the gut. I felt like someone completely knocked the wind out of me. When Dad died... it left a gaping hole in my chest that could never be filled. I will forever feel empty and lost without him.

I don't know how to live without him.

I don't want to; it's too hard.

Before I even realize what I'm doing, my fingers dial Athena's number, longing to hear her voice.

She picks up after the first ring. "Hello?" Athena's voice is groggy, like I may have woken her up.

It's already 10:23 p.m; I shouldn't have called so late. "I'm sorry. Did I wake you up?"

"It's fine. I was just dozing off. Is everything okay?" Athena asks, concern in her voice.

"Nothing." My voice was tired, low. "I just wanted to hear your voice."

CHAPTER 20

Athena:

I SAT IN THE CAR, RACKING my brain, wondering what on earth possessed me to agree to meet up with Dad today. Taking longer than necessary, I unbuckle my seatbelt, grab my purse, and head toward the coffee shop door.

As I walk into the crowded coffee shop, a whiff of coffee beans and freshly baked pastries hits my nose. With my stomach in knots, I can't help but feel queasy.

Even after all these years, it's almost as if nothing has changed.

Through the sea of people, I can easily pick him out of a crowd—it's in his stance, his posture, the way his shoulders slump over his coffee, stirring ever so casually. It makes me feel even sicker.

When Dad asked me to meet up with him, I agreed, but that doesn't mean I have to *like* it.

Dad smiles when he sees me, waving a little too enthusiastically. Reluctantly, I walk over to where he is sitting, pulling out the green metal chair across from him.

We sit in silence for a while as Dad gingerly sips his black coffee.

I notice that he ordered a drink for me too. The steaming cup of hot chocolate is tempting, but I push it away. I don't intend to be here long enough to drink it.

There's a crease in Dad's brow when he sees that the drink remains untouched; he even seems disappointed but doesn't say so.

Breaking the silence between us, I cut to the chase—stating my real reason for coming here in the first place. "Why did you stop replying to my letters?" I ask, years of irritation bleeding into my voice.

He furrows his brows as if he needs to process the question. "What letters?"

"Classic." Dad looks over at me with the world's greatest poker face. Somehow, he manages to look like he has no idea what I am talking about.

"Oh, okay, keep playing the victim all you want, but I'm not buying it," I fire back in disbelief.

There's absolutely no way he could not have seen my letters when *he* was the one who responded to them, well, that is, until he stopped.

"We're done here," I say, refusing to sit here any longer. I let him know that I've made up my mind.

"Athena, wait—" Dad calls out, trying to stop me from leaving.

Reaching into my bag, I pull out a ten-dollar bill from my wallet, slapping it onto the wooden coffee table. "That should be enough to cover my drink."

Dad looks like he is in shock as I swiftly get up from my seat, pushing open the heavy metal shop doors without looking back.

• • ⚭ • •

I make it home faster than I intended to; with my patience wearing thin, I feel like I am hanging on by a thread. I'm glad I didn't tell anyone I was meeting up with Dad today—the fewer expectations, the better. We have been let down enough.

I am angry and frustrated, but not enough to cry about it.

I wouldn't call myself a crier. I cried a lot more when I was younger, but as I got older, I came to see that crying doesn't solve anything. If anything, it only adds to the pain, giving you a major headache. So, I don't cry.

I refuse to cry.

In moments like these, I know exactly what I need. In desperate need of fresh air, I leave the car at home and go for a walk.

• • ∽ • •

The branches from the trees cast a faint shadow over the stone-covered path. The sun is warm and soothing as it warms my skin. I soak it all in. My head is flooded with useless thoughts, but I don't dare to let myself be distracted by them. Pulling out my phone from my pocket, I scroll through my favorite songs, settling on Good Thing by Kelahni. This song never fails to put me in a good mood.

The warm breeze caresses my face as I close my eyes and begin to count.

55...

60...

65...

70...

75...

80...

It takes only 98 steps to get there.

85...

I stop at the bubble tea shop next door. The "Royal Tea" sign is written in white cursive letters on a black backdrop. The door chimes as I open it.

As I walk up to the counter, Diamond greets me with a smile. I smile in return as Diamond asks, "Same order as usual?"

I nod in agreement, and Diamond turns to make our drinks. My mouth waters as I watch her make it; I can almost taste it.

"Here you are. One honeydew milk tea, and one winter melon Boba tea," Diamond says. Heading over to grab the drinks, I tell her, "Thank you, Diamond, you are the best." Cradling the drinks in my hands, I stroll to the pet daycare next door.

• • ∽ • •

As I open the door, Violet spots me first. "You are a lifesaver!" She's trapped under a big furry friend, and by the looks of it, he is not giving in.

I snap a photo of it for my amusement, and Violet snarls at me. "Hey, remember me? The one trapped under a 100lb Labrador? Mind helping me out?" she says, annoyed.

The dog wags his tail side to side, enjoying himself.

Setting the drinks down on the counter, I crouch down on my knees. "Hi, boy. Is V giving you a hard time today?"

He wags his tail and barks in response.

I'll take that as a yes.

"Oh, you poor thing having to put up with her *all* day." I lean over to pet him. Prince loves it when I scratch behind his ears.

Prince rolls over so I can scratch his belly, setting Violet free.

Violet scoffs. "For the record, I didn't give anyone a hard time. Trouble over here didn't like it very much when I told him it was time for him to take a bath."

Laughing at his problem-solving skills, I ask, "Is this true, buddy? You sat on her so you could avoid your bath?"

Prince barks.

Well, at least he knows how to admit when he was wrong.

Violet grabs her bubble tea and gulps it down in almost one go.

"Slow your roll, or you'll choke," I warn her, taking a slurp of mine. It is tangy and sweet, just the way I like it.

"I was feeling so dehydrated. You showed up at the perfect time."

"What time is your shift done?"

Violet glances at her watch. "In about ten minutes."

"Great. I'm coming over."

• • ☙ • •

"Athena!!! So good to see you. Come in, come in." Anya kisses me on both cheeks and wraps me in a warm hug.

"Good to see you too, Anya," I say, hugging her back.

Anya gives the best hugs.

Anya is a Hungarian word for mom. Violet's Mom is more or less my mom, too, so the name felt well suited to her.

"How come when I get home, I never get such a warm greeting from you?" Violet eyes the two of us.

"Because I like her more than you," Anya says.

Pinching her nose, Anya hits Violet with a towel telling her she stinks and to hurry up and take a shower.

"Mom!" Violet rubs her arm. "Stop hitting me; you're so mean."

"Maybe I'll be nicer once you're clean. Go."

Chuckling at the two of them, I make my way over to the kitchen to fetch us some snacks for the movie we're going to watch later.

"Come. Sit." Anya moves me over to the kitchen table. She scoops out some food for me, complaining that I am too skinny and need to eat more.

I'm not really in the mood to eat, though.

"I'm not hungry. I had a big lunch."

Seeing through my lie, Anya doesn't take no for an answer. "Then force yourself to eat it, anyway. For *me*."

I obediently oblige, stuffing my face with heaping spoonfuls of food. No matter how much I eat, it doesn't manage to fill the hole burrowing inside of me.

Anya hands me a glass of water, telling me to slow down or I'll choke. I gulp down the water, then place it on the table to take a breather.

Anya cups my face in her hands. "When your heart is aching, a warm cooked meal is the best medicine."

Unable to meet her eyes, I look down at my hands. "You were always able to do that." My voice is soft. I look up into her warm brown eyes. "To see how I feel without me telling you."

"I've known you for over 18 years. You have always been so dear to me." Anya smiles at me. "When we were going through our rough patch, you were always there to lend a helping hand. We may not be blood-related, but we are *family*. I'll always be here for you, sweetie."

I hug her. Anya rubs my hair soothingly, as a mom would. "Oh sweetie, it's going to be okay," she says.

. . ✿ . .

During the middle of the movie, I start laughing uncontrollably. It's not even a part that is supposed to be remotely funny. The main couple in the movie broke up, and the main girl is bawling her eyes out because she misses him.

I know it's supposed to be sad, but for some strange reason, I can't bring myself to empathize with her.

I'm a horrible human being, I know.

Violet is starting to look worried that something is seriously wrong with me. "Are you actually... laughing right now?" Violet says, drying the tears from her own eyes.

I guess I'm just heartless.

"Are you okay?" Violet asks, sounding concerned.

I don't know why she is making something out of *nothing*; I am perfectly fine.

"Of course, I'm okay. Why do you ask?" I turn to face her.

"Well, maybe because you seem a little *hysterical*?" Violet says, trying to get me to see her point.

This makes me laugh even harder. "Me? Hysterical? Oh, please." I continue laughing, holding my stomach and pointing at the TV screen. I try to talk, but no audible words come out.

The next thing I know, my pearls of laughter turn watery as tears fill my eyes.

I promised myself that I wouldn't cry. "I..." The tears come pouring out of my eyes. "I—I'm angry... so angry at him... for hurting me."

Giving in, feeling exhausted and defeated, I break down and cry, clutching my chest. "You know what hurts me the most?" I ask, my voice wobbling.

"I *want* to hate him." I laugh a little, bitterness in my tone when I say, "I want to hate him so bad."

Violet comes to sit beside me, rubbing my back. My voice is small when I admit, "But I can't... I just *can't*... because... he's the one I love the most."

I heave heavy sobs, my body shaking as I cry uncontrollably, with Violet consoling me.

CHAPTER 21

Athena:

FOR AS LONG AS I CAN remember, it has always been us, the three musketeers. We all grew up here together up until we finished high school. Josiah and his family moved to Australia shortly after we graduated. Naturally, because of the distance, we don't get to see each other all that often. Nonetheless, Josiah has and will always be a part of our family. When we decided to go on this trip together, I was thrilled to finally get to spend some time together, just like old times.

Where are we going? No clue, but anywhere that isn't *here* sounds pretty good to me right now.

With the windows down, I lean my head out the window and, for the first time in a long time, feel refreshed and at ease. The sun bleeds into the open road as we just drive—destination unknown.

.. ৵ ..

"Are we there yet?" Josiah groans, asking again for the 16th time in the past hour and 20 minutes.

Yes, I've been keeping count.

Josiah needs to zip it before Violet loses it. Josiah starts poking her in the arm. "Are. We. There. Yet?" Josiah continues to whine. One more poke, and Violet snaps her head around.

"Get out," Violet says through gritted teeth. Violet can be scary when she wants to be, but Josiah never learns.

"But we're going 85 miles an hour down the highway in the middle of nowhere. You can't be serious." Josiah smiles affectionately at her, thinking she is kidding.

"Did I stutter?"

Josiah coughs into his sleeve, saying the window must be open. He feels a cold chill run up his spine. Violet's eyes are ice-cold. He slowly slumps down in the passenger seat. "Okay. Okay. I'll behave."

Yeah, right, Josiah is a pot-stirrer. Do you know how some people can catch the wind of a situation and immediately try to stop it from escalating further? Josiah, on the other hand, can never catch a hint. That or he refuses to acknowledge it. Either way, he tends to irritate a lot of people for this very reason.

. . ᘓ . .

Eventually, we reach our destination. Or at least we decide it is because it's been six hours, and we feel pretty tired and hungry. My stomach feels like it is about to eat itself. I haven't eaten anything since this morning, which feels almost eons away. Mind you, the worst person to make go hungry is the one behind the wheel. Let's just say that I have never prayed as often in my life as I did today, praying to make it there alive. If someone does not put food in Violet's mouth, she just might eat one of us.

. . ᘓ . .

After eating, we stop at a flea market. My eyes scan through the quiet bohemian store decorated in bright colours. Various shades of scarlet, burgundy, and fuchsia cover the entire store. I can't help but be drawn to its colourful interior. I take note of the leather straps hanging up on the spindle in front of me. Touching the dark brown leather guitar straps, I'm reminded that Caiden's has worn out, fraying at the edges. I wonder if Caiden would make fun of me for buying him a gift. Or maybe he would have a huge smile light up his face.

Why are you thinking about his smile right now? Gosh, get it together, Athena.

I shake the thought out of my head. When I turn around, Josiah is staring inquisitively at me. "Geez, what are you doing?"

"I should be asking you that." Josiah nods towards the guitar strap in my hand. "Who's that for?" I pretend to be busy, fiddling with the sunglasses on the display beside me.

"It's for Caiden, isn't it?"

The only way he would know that is if... I'm going to kill Violet.

Josiah gives me a knowing look. Oh, how I hate that look. "Stop that."

Josiah gives me a 'who me?' face. "Stop what?"

"Wipe that annoying smirk off your face."

Josiah's eyes widen. "Shh, not another word," he says, putting a finger to his lips.

Josiah snaps a picture of me, so I whack the back of his head. "It's astonishing, it is," he says, looking at the camera.

I glare at Josiah, but he's undeterred. Instead, he starts to tear up. "I never thought I'd live to see the day"—he wipes his fake tears—"that Athena... fell in love." Pushing his camera toward me, he says, "Hold my camera. I need a tissue." He continues to fake cry into his hands.

Josiah is full of theatrics.

People walk by and point at us. They believe he is crying; they whisper as they pass by.

Then Josiah sniffles up his fake tears, takes a bow, and says overdramatically, "And scene."

"Ugh, actors."

"This is why they pay me the big bucks."

"That reminds me, where is *my* gift?"

"You're looking at it." Josiah gestures up and down to himself as the grand prize.

I scoff at that. "Send it back. I don't want it."

· · ✑ · ·

After we leave the store, the three of us stroll through the busy, lively streets. The decadent smell of fried fish and baked goods lingers in the air. We grab freshly squeezed smoothies from a tall guy in a huge straw hat. I gulp down the mango pineapple smoothie, and soon after, I need to pee. Violet and Josiah stick around, drinking their smoothies on the bench, waiting for me.

I'm walking out of the bathroom when I see Violet silently staring back at Josiah as anger flashes across his face.

What did I miss?

I was gone for all of five minutes. I'm about to ask what happened when Josiah speed walks over to me with Violet slowly tagging along behind him.

I nudge Violet in the arm. "What was *that* all about?"

Violet stares at Josiah. "Nothing."

Okay, that was weird.

· · ✑ · ·

I take my time collecting gifts to bring back for my family, Ashley, and Isabella. Mom wanted me to get her a dining set. I think she has one too many, but who am I to judge? I'm the one with a massive collection of books that I don't read. Sky wanted me to look for a polaroid camera. She mainly just wants it to be put on the floating wall shelf in her bedroom. "It's for the aesthetic," Sky keeps telling me.

I find a nice polaroid camera in pastel pink, her favorite color, and for Mom, an aquamarine blue laced with a golden copper dining set that I hope she likes. Ashley loves fuzzy slippers, so I got her a pair of white and black panda slippers. For Isabella, rhinestone-studded headphones.

· · ✑ · ·

The second that I step my foot into the doorway, Sky comes bounding down the stairs. No hi or hello, she goes straight to, "Did you get it?"

I pull the gifts I got for each of them out of my duffel bag. "Why, hello to you too," I say, handing her the bag with her name on it.

Sky screams. "This is the same one I saw on Pinterest! Thank you!"

Mom loves the bright colours in the dining set I got for her; she hurries to pop them in the dishwasher so we can use them for dinner tonight. I know I *should* stay for dinner since I just got home, but... I was hoping to stop by the Alshaaers' house tonight before it gets too late. Or maybe I'll just head over tomorrow after work.

I still have to unpack.

· · ❧ · ·

Since Sky was already in a good mood, maybe now would be a good time to talk to her. I saunter to her bedroom, knocking on the door. "Come in," Sky says, so I open the door walking in.

"To what do I owe this pleasure, sister dear?" Sky asks, spinning around in her chair.

"I have a question."

"Do tell." Sky folds her hands across her chest.

"What do *you* do when you like a boy?"

"I tell him," Sky replies simply.

It's not always that simple, though. "And if he *doesn't* like you back?"

"I'll have to kill him," she replies, sipping her tea.

The mind of a child is truly a wonderful thing.

· · ❧ · ·

After we eat dinner, I find out that Sky has made plans to go over to Isabella's house tonight. Perfect, now I can use driving her there as an excuse to go. Not that I need one or anything, but it would avoid those suspicious looks that I know I would get if I were to mention going over there.

"I'll drive you," I say, putting my plate in the dishwasher.

Sky gives me a contemplating look. "What's in it for you?"

"Oh, don't you worry your pretty little head about it." I pat Sky's hair; she's not pleased with the adoring sister act.

"Ohhh," Sky taps her chin. "I see what's going on here..."

"Time to go!" I say, rushing Sky out the door.

. . ∽✤∽ . .

When we arrive, Sky and Isabella scurry off to her bedroom, leaving me, Ashley, and Caiden in the living room. "This is for you," I say, giving Ashley the panda slippers, hoping she will like them.

Ashley puts them on right away. "These are adorable; I love them."

I put the bag for Isabella with the bedazzled headphones on the table. I will give them to her later.

Caiden is eyeing me expectantly, probably wondering if I have a gift for him, too.

I shove his bag with the leather guitar strap toward him. "Don't go feeling *special* or anything." A smile grows on Caiden's face. "I only got this because I just *happened* to see it at the cashier when I was buying everyone else's gifts."

Caiden still has that goofy grin on his face. "Aw, Athena, I'm touched," he says, clasping a hand to his chest.

"Don't go getting a big head over it."

Caiden opens the gift bag, pulling out the brown leather guitar strap, running his fingers along the edges, admiring it. "This is perfect. I love it. Thank you. I'm going to try it out right now."

. . ∽✤∽ . .

Caiden pulls out his guitar from beside the bed in his room, putting on the new guitar strap I got him.

"I'm working on learning to play this song," he says. "Do you want to hear it?"

"Sure," I say, noting that Caiden looks so peaceful sitting there, strumming away on his guitar.

The melody sounds vaguely familiar.

As he continues to play, I think I can make out what song it is. "Is that... The Scientist by Coldplay?"

Caiden's mouth curves up into a smile. "Yes, it is."

"This is one of my favourite songs." Glancing up at him, I beg him to continue. "Can you show me how to play it?" I ask, moving to sit beside him on the couch.

"Sure." Caiden hands me the guitar, showing me which cords to play. Fumbling, I try my best to follow along as he moves my hands to the right chords. Feeling a little flustered, I refuse to make eye contact with him.

Caiden chuckles. "Are you laughing at me?" Appalled by his behavior, I punch him in the arm.

"No, no, not at all," he insists, throwing his head back and cackling with laughter.

"It's just that there's this face you make when you focus on something." Caiden turns to look at me. "It's simply adorable."

My lips curve up into a smile. There's this glimmer in his eyes as he smiles back at me. Reaching over, he tenderly places a hand on my cheek as if he's about to kiss me.

Suddenly, he pulls back, a strange look on his face. "What's... what's wrong?" I ask, puzzled.

He shifts uncomfortably. "I... I'm sorry."

"What are you sorry for? It's fine. I—"

"We can't do this." Caiden's voice is now stern and cold.

"Do what? What can't you do?"

"I can't..." He trails off, looking at his feet, then glancing back at me for a moment. "I can't like you."

I can't help but laugh.

This is ridiculous. Is he going to tell me that he's secretly married or something?

"Athena," he says, distracting me from my thoughts.

"I'm sick." Caiden looks me dead in the eyes, so I can see he is not joking.

I feel like the wind has been knocked out of me.

"What...? How—how is that possible?" My stomach clenches.

"I have MS," he says, sounding surprisingly calm.

My head is spinning, trying to make sense of it all.

I'm at a loss for words. How can this be?

I want to cry.

I want to scream.

MS... That's what Evan's mom has. She's... in a wheelchair now, barely hanging on. But that doesn't mean... maybe there's still a chance that...

"You're still young..." I fight the lump forming in my throat. "We can... we can work through this. Maybe there's something that can be done." I search his face, begging for answers.

"I want to help in any way that I can. You don't have to go through this alone," I ramble on, hoping to get through to him.

Suddenly his eyes cloud over. His jaw sets as he stares off into the distance. An uncomfortable silence passes between us before he blurts out, "I need you to leave."

I wince at his harsh words. "I'm sorry I—"

"Now." Caiden's demeanor has changed. His eyes are cold and distant.

Feeling lost and dejected, I stumble out of his room, heading for the front door.

"Leaving so soon?" Ashley calls out as I approach the door. As tears threaten to fall from my eyes, I hide my face and solemnly wave goodbye.

CHAPTER 22
Caiden:

I COULDN'T LET HER see me like this.

A piercing pain rips through me, sending sharp electric shocks throughout my body. My legs feel like limp noodles as I try my best to move them but fail miserably. Falling to my knees, I beg my body to work with me as the sharp pain jolts through my arms and legs.

Groaning, I scan the room for my phone.

It's on the desk in the far corner of my bedroom.

Clutching my hands around the chair leg, I try to use it as leverage to knock the phone down off the desk by slamming the chair into it, hoping the force will knock my phone down. Thankfully, the phone eventually falls to the ground, bouncing as it hits the hardwood floor—my hand trembles as I'm finally able to reach it. Leaning on the chair for support, I try to stand up, but my vision blurs like my eyes are covered with a thick layer of Vaseline.

The chair comes crashing down with me as my legs give way, and my head knocks into the corner of the desk. I'm left lying lifeless on the cold, hard floor.

Tears sting my eyes as I lay there, afraid.

The doctors told me that my MS could progress rapidly at any given time. I have a rare case that does not have a cure. I've accepted that.

The fact that I won't live very long—it's inevitable. But Athena... she makes me want to *live*.

"Caiden!" I can hear my Mom yelling as she frantically sprints up the stairs to my room. Opening the door, she looks at me with teary eyes.

Mom quickly composes herself, bends down, and soothingly pats my hair. "It's okay, sweetie. It's going to be okay."

Knowing I can't get up alone, Mom slowly helps to lift me, easing me back onto the bed.

CHAPTER 23

Athena:

IN MY CAR, AN INCOMING text message from Ashley pops up on the phone.

Ashley: Don't worry about Sky. I will bring her home.

Athena: Thank you so much.

I feel guilty that I completely forgot about Sky.

With a million and one questions threatening to eat me alive, I search up MS to see what information I can find. I'm searching for cures and treatments when I come across- "It's a ruthless disease that attacks the body's nervous system. You will eventually lose control over your body and become paralyzed, which shortens your life expectancy. Treatments and medicine only help to slow down MS symptoms, but depending on how severe your case of MS is, it can take a turn for the worst and speed up at any given time."

· · ⌀ · ·

I call Violet when I get home, and by now, I'm crying uncontrollably. Before I can even get any words out, she says, "Be there in ten."

Violet doesn't stop to knock on my door. She flings it open, demanding, "Alright, who's face do I need to smash in?" A baseball bat dangles from her hand.

"V, calm down. Let's be rational about this."

"Calm down? No, I will *not* calm down." Then a look of realization passes on Violet's face. "It was Caiden, wasn't it?"

I don't respond, which Violet takes to mean yes.

131

"Okay, wow. He dared to break your heart; I will break his—"

"V—" I cover her mouth with my hand, muffling her voice. "Quiet down, will you? The last thing I need is for Alex to hear us." When I think she is calmer, I let go.

"Seriously?" Violet puts both hands on her hips, not impressed. "You're seriously worried about *his* safety right now? No, not acceptable. He hurt you; he has to pay."

Alex would flip out if he found out I was crying over a guy.

"On a scale of 1-10, how bad would it be if—"

"At least a 20." Violet knows exactly what I'm thinking, and she knows Alex's temper just as well as I do.

Violet glances at me like she knows there is more to the story. "You're hiding something from me, aren't you?" She moves to sit beside me on the bed. "What is it you're not telling me?"

I want to tell her everything. I do, but I don't even have the words to describe how I'm feeling right now. "Nothing. I just... I just need some sleep."

"No, what you need is to come with me. We're not going to let you just sit here and wallow in self-pity."

"Please," I plead with her, "I just want... to be alone right now." Violet wraps me up in a hug, saying she doesn't want to leave me, but she will wait until I'm ready to talk about it.

I feel guilty for pushing her away like that when she came over here to comfort me. "Thank you, and I'm sorry."

"Don't be. Just remember this when I'm being a pain in the butt later." When Violet lets go, I force myself to smile. She picks up her bat and walks away, closing the door behind her.

• • ❧ • •

Sometime later, fat raindrops trickle down my windowpane, and bursts of thunder and lightning soon follow. The pouring rain sounds like mu-

sic to my ears. Shots of lightning and the rumbling thunder are somehow very comforting.

Not even bothering to grab a jacket, I make my way outside.

Soaked to the bone, my clothes cling to my skin, the cold, wet raindrops biting into my face and hair.

I'm grateful to drown in something other than my thoughts.

I close my eyes, wishing and hoping that none of this happened,
that I would open them again and find out it was all just a really bad
dream.

One where Caiden wasn't sick.

Dragging myself back inside the house, I open the door to my bedroom, the water dripping off my clothes and hair, but I just don't have
the energy to shower. Instead, I collapse onto the bed, rolling over and
closing my eyes.

. . ৵৹ . .

The next morning, Mom opens my bedroom door, then quickly covers
her nose, disgusted by the stench rolling off me. "What smells like a wet
dog in here?" Stripping off the covers, she sees me lying there, curled up
in a ball, with bags under my eyes.

"I'm tired." I groan, wanting to be left alone. Mom pushes me into
the shower, telling me to get rid of that smell before I come downstairs.

I drag my body into the shower. While in there, I let the warm water wash me clean as I try not to think about Caiden. That plan doesn't
work, though.

All I can think about is him.

. . ৵৹ . .

Downstairs, I walk over to the fridge to get a glass of water. Violet is
here with us; she usually comes to join us for breakfast on the weekends.

Sky has a horrified expression on her face. "Why do you look like you've been run over by a truck?" Violet slaps a hand over Sky's mouth.

I look at Violet. "Do I look that bad?"

"No, sweetie, of course not." Violet smooths my still-damp hair.

Sky is right I note, looking at myself in the hallway mirror. I *do* look like I got run over by a truck. The bags and dark circles around my eyes make it look like I have aged overnight.

Sky shakes her head. "What you *mean* to say is that she looks like a hot mess." Violet kicks Sky in the shins.

Sky yelps from the pain, glaring at Violet. "Violence is not necessary."

· · ✦ · ·

That evening, Mom calls me and Alex to come to the living room. There is something she wants to tell us. I've had enough unpleasant surprises these past few weeks, and I'm not sure I am ready to hear another one.

"Athena, Alex, come here, please. We need to talk," Mom says, patting the seat beside her on the couch.

I think back to the day Mom told us that Dad left home. She sat us down right here on this green couch. All Mom said was that they were trying to work some things out. They fought, and that's why Dad left. Of course, I loved my Mom to death, but I was a daddy's girl. I'd follow him wherever he went. Anywhere you found him, I wasn't more than a few steps behind.

I kept telling myself that it was *just* a fight.

Dad would eventually come to his senses and return home.

There wasn't a day that passed that I didn't wait for him. With each passing day, I'd tell myself, "He's coming tomorrow." I was sure of it. Dad just needed to blow off some steam. He'd be back.

He had to be.

Days turned into weeks, weeks into months, and then years. Six years. I waited for him relentlessly every day for six years, all the while growing more angry and bitter with each passing year. Dad abandoned me when I needed him most, so I hated him for it.

It wasn't until now that we heard the full story.

Mom goes on to tell us what happened, the whole story of what went down before he had left home that day.

Dad got injured on the construction job where he was working. He had a bad fall that broke his hip, sprained his wrist, and fractured his rib and spine. His body kept getting used to the pain medicine after a while, which made them no longer effective, so in time, Dad had to go on some powerful medication for the pain.

Because of his injuries, he couldn't work.

Mom picked up more shifts at the job she was working. At the time, she worked for a cleaning business, doing office cleaning. This way, she would work while Dad stayed home to watch us.

But Dad started to feel incompetent as a father because he could no longer provide for his family, all the while we were struggling to make ends meet. On the other hand, Mom felt guilty that she couldn't be at home to take care of us.

So, this caused them to fight constantly about anything and *everything*.

That's when Dad started drinking. It was his way of drowning out the pain he was feeling. When Mom saw how addicted he was becoming, unable to go a day without chugging down a six-pack of alcohol, she begged him to go to rehab to fix it before it got even worse. Dad agreed and promised to get help.

And then the lying started...

Lying about drinking and then drinking because he felt guilty for *lying*.

"Then one day, he went to pick you kids up from school after drinking. You were in kindergarten at the time. I didn't know your dad was coming and had already gone ahead and switched my shift to be back in time to pick you up." Mom continues to tell us what happened next.

· · ⁓ · ·

Dad had stumbled into the parking lot, unable to stand up straight. "Are you drunk?" Mom had asked him in disbelief at what she was seeing.

"No, I'm fine."

"Fine? No, you are *not* fine!" Mom had exploded on him, unable to hold back her anger. "You are *fine* putting your kid's life at risk?! Are you out of your *mind*?!"

I had no idea all that had been going on.

All I remember from that day was being so excited to see Dad that I immediately ran over to hug him. "Daddy!" Whereas Alex had slung his backpack over his shoulder and opened the car door, not bothering to say a word to anyone.

I remember the car ride home had been uncomfortably silent, with Mom and Dad refusing to say a word to each other. I sensed they must have had a fight, but I didn't think anything of it. I just thought all parents fought at times, right?

Alex had looked over at them, his brows knitted together.

When we got home, Alex complained of chest pain. "It hurts! My chest hurts so bad..." Alex sniffled. "Make it stop... make it go away."

Mom had hurried to check on him, gathering Alex in her arms. "It's okay, sweetie. Come here."

"It hurts..."

Even at that age, Alex had known our family was falling apart, and it was a heartache that none of us were prepared to take.

· · ⁓ · ·

Mom takes our hands in hers. "We both made some decisions that we regret. We are only *human*; it's natural for us to make mistakes. What matters most is how you deal with it. It's what you do after that *counts*. Your father has changed. He acknowledges his mistakes and wants to own up to them. Maybe at that time he wasn't ready to make those changes, but he is now. So, I guess the real question is, are you?"

Alex scoffs. "He had a *problem*?" His tone was frigid, and his eyes ice cold. "Well, then he should have *fixed* it. He could have stuck it out. He just took the easy way out." Not being able to stand giving it another thought, he leaves.

Sighing, Mom watches Alex walk away. I guess this didn't go over as well as she thought it would.

Mom fixes her gaze on me, probably wondering what my take is on all of this. "That's great, Mom," I say, my voice dripping with sarcasm. "Good for you for taking the high road. I'm sorry, but I'm not you. I wouldn't have forgiven him."

Dad just threw us away too easily, and I can't forgive him for that.

. . ✿ . .

When I get back upstairs to my room, Josiah is there with Violet, talking in a hushed tone. If that's not suspicious, I don't know what is.

Never mind the fact that Josiah came over, and I had no idea he was here.

Either way, I'm happy to see them. So glad to have allies right now.

"Hey, what's up? Are you guys talking about me over there?" I ask teasingly, sitting down beside Violet. "Busted," Josiah says with a weak laugh. "Do you remember the first time we met?"

"Of course," I respond.

Violet smiles, looking at me as she remembers the fond memory of the day the three of us met. "It was back in kindergarten, remember?"

It was the day we had our first parent-teacher interviews. Everyone had both Mom and Dad show up, smiling like perfect little happy families. We were the only three in the whole class who didn't have Dads.

"The look of pity Ms. Summers gave us when she looked at us was pure horror." He shudders at the thought of it.

"But then..." Violet takes each of our hands in hers. "That was a glorious day because that was the moment we became best friends."

Why do I feel like there is some kind of underlying reason Josiah and Violet are bringing up this story? "What are you getting at?" I peer curiously at my friends, wondering what is going on. Violet and Josiah exchange worried glances.

Josiah hesitantly moves over to sit closer to me. "A, you know you mean the world to me, right?"

"Yes, but—" I start

"So, remember that and listen carefully to what I'm about to tell you." Josiah glances over at Violet again. "Knowing that we only have your best interests at heart." He takes a deep breath, steadying himself for what he is about to say. "It's about your Dad."

I take in a sharp breath; he is the absolute last person I want to talk about right now.

"You and I both know that we all hate his guts for what he did to you, Alex, and your Mom. He never should have treated you that way. But we also know that at least he's *making* an effort to come back into your lives." Josiah puts a hand on my arm. "Where are *our* dads, Athena? They might as well have dropped off the face of the earth because they have *never* come back for us. But, Athena, your dad came back. For *you*."

"Well, it's just a little too late for that."

"I get that. But what I don't get is why you're acting like this."

I crinkle my brows. "Like what?"

"Like a coward."

I feel like Josiah just slapped me right across the face.

"You hated your dad for running away and not being brave enough to face his problems. But look at what you are doing. Like him, you

are running away because you are scared. This isn't like you. What happened to feisty, say-whatever-is-on-her-mind Athena?"

"That's not... I'm not—" I shake my head in disbelief.

Long after Violet and Josiah leave, I find myself staring outside my
bedroom window, watching the leaves fall from the oak tree. Josiah's
words were a bitter pill to swallow. The reason why those words stung
so much was that they rang true.

I am a hypocrite and a coward.

All I cared about was being right. Because I knew that otherwise,
my mind wouldn't be at ease, it would be my fault for relentlessly
choosing to be unhappy.

CHAPTER 24
Caiden:

I JUMP OUT OF BED WITH the unsettling feeling that I forgot to do something important. Groaning in pain from getting up too quickly, I try to stand up, and my head spins. As I take a deep breath, my side aches from where I fell. Lifting the bottom of my shirt, I can see a purple bruise starting to form.

It hurts, but it is manageable.

Looking at the clock, I see that it's already 8:00 a.m. That's right. I was supposed to meet up with Damon at the tennis court today—at 7:00. I'm already an *hour* late.

Oh, shoot.

I lace up my running shoes as quickly as I can, then head for the door.

.. ⌒⌒ ..

By the time I arrive at the tennis court, Damon is standing by the gate, a grim look on his face.

It's official. I am a horrible human being. The worst-friend-ever award goes to Caiden Alshaaer. "I'm so sorry, man."

"Are you?" Drew looks unimpressed by my late arrival. "You *forgot*, didn't you?"

"I'm sorry." I don't mean to be a bad friend.

Damon walks off, ignoring my apology. Turning the latch on the gate, he picks up the tennis ball, taking a swing with the racquet. "No, it's okay. I'm used to it by now. I'm easily forgotten."

"No, it's cool." Damon puts the racquet down, a hint of frustration in his tone. "Dude, I'm just going to come right out and say it." He pauses, looking at me. "Am I your friend?"

Yes, without a doubt. Why would he even have to ask that?

"Of course," I say with confidence. Damon has been my best friend for years.

Damon shakes his head. "Because a friendship is supposed to be a two-way street, man."

I blink, not understanding where all this is coming from.

"*I'm* always the one doing all the talking. I mean, you know everything there is to know about me, from my sad, pathetic love life to my horrid relationship with my mother. But you..." He trails off like he needs a minute to get his thoughts together first. "I feel like I don't even know you at all. All I know about your dad is that..."

Even after so much time has passed, it hasn't gotten any easier to talk about it.

A part of me wanted to, but then I think it would be cruel of me to unleash that burden on someone else.

"Maybe talking..." Damon's tone is softer now. "Opening up about it can be... therapeutic. Have you ever thought about or considered going to therapy?"

"I'm fine," I reply, although by now, even I no longer believe it.

We play a few rounds of tennis until we are both too tired to play anymore. Damon even drops the subject for a while, which I'm grateful for because, to be honest, even if he asked me to confide in him, I honestly don't even know what I'd say.

. . ⌘ . .

As we are leaving the tennis court, Damon turns to me. "I mean, am I *crazy,* or is there something wrong here?"

I know that he means well, and he's only looking out for me, and I do appreciate his support. But I'm too broken, too far gone to be fixed.

I smile, but my heart's not in it. "Bold of you to assume that you were ever *sane,* to begin with."

At that, Damon hits the ball with the tennis racket, purposely sending the ball into the trees behind the metal wire fence. "I *must* be crazy," he says, shaking his head. "Otherwise, I can't understand why on earth I still put up with you."

Pointing to the trees, Damon tells me, "It's only fair that you go get that for all the emotional turmoil you put me through."

Honestly, he's got a valid point. I'm not the easiest guy to put up with.

Even *I'm* tired of dealing with myself. I am so happy that I have a loyal friend like Damon.

CHAPTER 25
Caiden:

THERE IS NOT A SINGLE day that goes by that I do not think of him. Every time I walk by Dad's old room is a reminder of the way his eyes crinkled when he smiled and just how much I miss having him around.

Lately, I wake up in cold sweats, my body violently shaking—not from my MS, but the gut-wrenching guilt. I keep reliving it, over and over again, my dad's face so vividly ingrained in my mind.

My chest burns and aches as if my heart is being gouged out with fire.

Oh, how I wish I hadn't been so selfish and persistent.

I promised myself that day that I would never act so selfishly again.

With the plethora of thoughts weighing on my mind, I need to find an outlet, a safe space. Hoping to clear my mind, I make my way to the pottery room.

"Pot of Gold" has become a home away from home for me.

I found myself instantly drawn to the quiet and still candor of the place. Late evening is the best time to stop by because hardly anyone ever comes by at that time, leaving me all alone in the big spacious room. Ceramic and clay marbled pieces, ranging from ash gray to aquamarine blue, line the walls, filling a space on the oak shelves around the golden-lit room.

Picking up the brown wooden stool in the corner, I try to focus my attention on the clay mold in front of me, carefully forming the clay pieces so that the body has an even thickness.

It's of no use because all I can see is her.

Forcing my thoughts back to the clay, my hands move up and down in a circular motion, shaping the clay into a bowl shape. Again, my mind flashes back to the look on Athena's face, the pain in her eyes, and the weight of her gaze before she walked away.

As my mind continues to drift, my hands become more unsteady. The clay starts to crumble and lose shape, and I struggle to regain its structure and my composure.

With anger seeping through my veins, I fling open the wooden cupboard door, sending the rest of my finished pottery pieces hurling onto the floor—shards of broken ceramic spew out all over the ground.

Hot red blood trickles down my arm to my legs; I am desensitized to the pain.

CHAPTER 26
Caiden:

"CAIDEN!" ISABELLA'S shaking my shoulders, trying to get my attention. "You didn't hear us calling you?"

I must have been in a trance or something because I didn't hear a thing. My mind is... It's fair to say that I'm distracted.

Athena doesn't leave my mind.

Mom places a hand on the small of my back, concerned. "Is everything okay, sweetie?"

I lean back and close my eyes, sighing as Mom runs her fingers through my hair. "Yeah, I'm fine." Her fingers still for just a moment before she begins combing again.

Mom knows very well that I am far from fine.

She has that uncanny ability to read me like an open book. Lying is useless because nothing escapes her notice.

Isabella, completely oblivious to the situation, asks, "Hey, why hasn't Athena come over in a while? Did you guys fight?"

Mom gives Isabella a warning look that says not to press the matter any further.

I don't reply, not having enough energy to come up with a lie. "I'm going to go wash the dishes."

Mom brings her plate to the counter so I can wash it, but her food remains untouched; she barely even took a bite out of it.

Mom takes some saran wrap from the drawer to put over it, saying she will eat it later.

The problem is that's the *same* line I have been hearing for weeks now. When was the last time I saw her sit down and eat?

"Mom, it's 5:00, and you haven't had anything to eat all day."

Mom just shrugs it off as if it's not that big of a deal. "I'm not all that hungry these days, not much of an appetite."

That fact makes it even more concerning. There could be an underlying issue involved.

"That's not healthy. You need to eat something. I'll make an appointment with the doctor to get you checked out." I scroll for the doctor's number on my phone.

Mom places her hand on my arm. "No, sweetie, that won't be necessary. I feel fine."

Those words set me off, and I explode, yelling that she's not fine and needs to take better care of herself.

Mom flinches at my tone. "You know what? I've got these dishes." She stares back at me, her voice clipped. "Maybe you should go for a walk, get some air until you cool down."

Isabella shakes her head at me, mouthing, 'Shame on you.'

I should never have yelled at Mom like that.

My face falls. "I'm sorry I—"

"I know." Mom nods. Without me saying so, she always knows exactly how I feel.

. . ⌇ . .

I'm outside the house now, walking aimlessly, dragging my feet through the grass. The problem is that I think too much. I spend so much time wondering what the future will look like instead of focusing on what is right here in front of me now. I know. Sometimes I wish I could just press fast forward to see how this would end.

This fear of the unknown is killing me.

Head in my hands, I continue walking until I see another pair of feet wearing mustard yellow kicks. I look up to see Athena walking toward me.

My treacherous heart skips a beat when I see her but then falls when I notice the scowl on her face. "What are you so afraid of, exactly?" Athena asks, her arms crossed over her chest.

"You."

Athena just doesn't see it. We have no chance if what she wants is a serious relationship; it has no *future*. "What exactly would be the point in all of this?"

She told me she wanted to have a family, that she dreams of having boy and girl twins.

I can't make her dreams a reality.

Athena lets out a dry laugh, turning the question around on me. "Hold on a second. Do *I* not get a say in the matter?"

"What—"

"I wasn't finished." Worked up now, she gets louder. "Don't. I'm sick of your excuses. If you don't want to be with me, just say so. Don't just hide behind... your illness. I'm sorry, but if this is the kind of person you are, then good riddance because I never knew you could be so selfish.

Athena:

CAIDEN LOOKS LIKE I just slapped him across the face.

The second the words came out of my mouth, I wanted to take them back, say I didn't mean it. He looks stunned, at a loss for words, making me wish I could go back in time and stop myself to unsee the pained look on his face.

We stand there in the uncomfortable silence, with me being too prideful and stubborn to say I'm sorry.

"Come with me," Caiden says, tugging on my wrist.

"What?"

He turns my arm towards me, showing me the hefty bruise I got from when I fell on the way here.

I was too lost in thought to pay attention to where I was going when I tripped and fell on the sidewalk. "What happened here, and why didn't you address it? You should be more careful," Caiden says, adopting his parent-tone.

Still embarrassed by my outburst, I shrug him off. "I'm fine, okay? Let go."

"No, you're *not* fine. You're only pretending to be," Caiden suddenly yells, and I can tell that it isn't just my bruise making him this angry.

• • ❧ • •

Sitting me down on the couch, he pleads with me to sit still while he tends to the wound.

I stop resisting.

It's painstakingly silent as I watch how he carefully cleans and wraps the wound. Although it stings, I'm as silent as a mouse because even though it hurts... my heart hurts *ten* times more.

When Caiden's done, he tells me that the cream needs to be applied at least twice a day until it heals. "The bandage will need to be changed every few days," he says, holding the ointment and bandages in the palm of his hand.

Reaching for it, my hand lingers as I look back at him.

My heart squeezes in my chest as I scramble for something to say. I want to say that I'm sorry, but the damage has already been done.

It is far too late.

I lower my gaze, remove my hand from his, and mumble, "Thanks."

• • ᴄᴏʃᴏ • •

Upon arriving home, Mom yells from the kitchen, telling me to come to eat, but my stomach is in knots. I don't have much of an appetite.

"Thanks," I say on my way up to my bedroom. "But I'm not hungry."

Curling up in bed, I pull the sheets over my head, lost in thought. The truth is, I am scared.

I am scared to even look at him, worried that my eyes will betray me, portraying how I feel.

When Caiden was dressing my wound, all I wanted to do was hold on to him and not let go. My heart is crushed, shattered to pieces. What hurts the most is that we were over before we even *started*.

I scroll through the pictures I took of him that day at the park on my phone; Caiden laughing, Caiden with a huge smile on his face. "I'm sorry, Caiden, for the awful things I say to you."

Caiden has been nothing but kind to me, and yet I reacted so harshly.

How could I have called him out for being selfish when that's *exactly* what I was doing?

Alex was right; I am a hypocrite.

CHAPTER 27
Athena:

IT'S BASKETBALL SEASON, and in this house, you could say that my family is a bunch of basketball fanatics. Everyone huddles around the TV in the living room to watch the game. Collin and Alex look like zombies glued to the screen.

The doorbell rings.

"The pizza is here!" Rain jumps off the couch to get to the door without getting the pizza money first.

Collin had given Alex the pizza money earlier today.

"Alex, where did you put the pizza money?" Alex ignores me, so I wave a hand in front of his face. "Hello, earth to Alex. Pizza. Money."

"On the desk in my room," Alex says, shooing me off.

Walking into Alex's room, I search his desk. Where did he put it? I don't see it here.

I shuffle through the papers on his desk but accidentally knock over one of his toy action figures. I snicker to myself. Isn't he a little too old to still be playing with toys?

Reaching under the bed to pick it up, I see an open black box with... is that an envelope with my name on it?

I slide the box from under the bed, taking a closer look at it. Inside, I can see that it's filled to the brim with a bunch of handwritten letters labeled, "From: Athena To: Dad."

What are my letters doing here?

Alex walks into his bedroom. "Hey, did you find—" He stops short when he sees the letter in my hand.

"Were we not good enough for you? Was I not good enough? Did you not love me enough to stay?" I read aloud the words I wrote to Dad years ago.

"Care to explain why these letters are in *your* possession and not Dad's?" Fury in my eyes, I demand an explanation.

Mom and Collin walk in now, looking from me to Alex. "What is going on?" Mom says.

"Is there anything *else* you're hiding from me?" I look over at each of them defiantly.

Collin shifts uncomfortably, looking down at his feet the whole time. His eyes are glued to the floor as if he's searching for something.

I fold my arms over my chest. "Now is your chance." I turn to face Mom and Collin. "Do I *also* have a secret twin sister?"

"Sweetie—" Mom starts in an attempt to explain herself, but it's of no use because I am sick and tired of hearing excuses.

"You know what? I am *tired*. Tired of being treated like a fragile piece of glass."

"Hey, that's not fair," Alex interjects, putting a hand on my shoulder.

Shrugging him off, I laugh bitterly. "Oh, *you* want to talk about fair? Do you know what's not fair?

Finding out that for years you've been lied to."

Alex looks back at me with a tinge of guilt in his eyes. "I just wanted to protect you."

"I don't need protecting. I'm not..." I close my eyes for a moment before I continue, "I'm not that sad little girl who woke up in the middle of the night crying for her daddy."

Collin clears his throat. "You know what? It's been a long day." Putting an arm around Mom's shoulder, he says soothingly, "We're all just tired. Let's head to bed and talk it out first thing in the morning." Collin has this ridiculous smile on his face, but I see it in his eyes.

They plead for me to step down.

CHAPTER 28
Athena:

THE FOLLOWING DAY, Alex strolls down the stairs at 12:41 p.m. to join us for lunch at the kitchen table. "Look who's *finally* decided to grace us with his presence," Mom says.

Usually, we would all laugh, and I'd poke fun at Alex for sleeping the day away, but today... Today, I'm not in the mood to even be in the same place as him.

I'm still furious that he kept such a big secret from me for so long. Like what am I, two?

I'm not a child.

I'm an adult; I would have been able to handle it.

"Woah, what did the food do to you?" Alex asks when he sees me aggressively stabbing the steak in front of me.

"He wasn't brave enough to tell me the truth." I turn my attention to Alex now. "Remind you of anybody?" Rain and Sky look between Alex and me as we glare at each other.

I get up abruptly, saying that I have lost my appetite.

"What is your problem?" Alex says to my retreating back before I can make it past the living room to my room.

What—

What is my problem?

How about the fact that Alex just glosses over things? As if they didn't matter. This is what he does. He just acts like everything is okay when it's far from okay.

As far as Alex is concerned, it's spilled milk. The problem is over and done with, so I should get over it too. Never mind the fact that he has been... lying to me all this time.

I thought we were on the same side.

Obviously, I was wrong.

"Really?" I scoff, annoyed that he could be so clueless. "Why don't you use that brain of yours and think about it?"

Alex shoves me on the shoulder. "You need to calm down, alright?"

You know what? He wants a fight?

I'll give him one.

I throw the first punch, hitting him in his stomach. Alex pushes me back. Meanwhile, Mom is yelling, telling us to stop acting like kids and act our age.

Collin steps in. "If you're going to fight, do it properly."

"Collin!" Mom yells, outraged that he is encouraging it.

"What?" Collin hands us gloves and headgear. "Let them get it out of their system."

I lunge at Alex, but he knocks me down, grabs my waist, and throws me to the ground. I overpower him and clasp my hands around Alex's legs, straddling him, so he comes crashing down.

We have a brawl crashing into things, with Alex trying to get a hold of himself while I swing away. Just as I think I've found my footing, Alex catches me off guard and puts me in a headlock.

I surrender first, feeling exhausted and tired.

Tired of everything.

. . ॐ . .

Opening the door to my bedroom, I heave a heavy sigh. All I want is peace. Peace from the whirring thoughts spiraling in my mind.

Feeling broken and bruised, I squeeze my eyes shut, trying to silence the noise.

My phone dings.

A reminder that Josiah has an audition today.

Oh, right, I forgot to ask him how that went. I'll text him right now.

Athena: How'd the interview go?

Josiah video calls me right away.

"Great, obviously!" he says, a huge smile on his face. "I blew their socks off."

"Of course, you'd say so." I laughed, rolling my eyes.

"So, you and Alex are still fighting?"I shoot him a look. "What do you think?"

Josiah nods. "You just don't get it, do you?"

Clearly, I've missed something here. "Get what?"

"Alex has *always* been the one to protect you," Josiah says.

"Yeah, well, maybe I don't need to be protected," I say, sitting up and adjusting the pillow behind my back.

"No, it's not meant as an insult. Alex *knows* you could protect yourself if you had to. But it's because he feels guilty for not being able to do anything the day your dad left." I'm not sure how I feel about hearing about all this.

Why would Alex...

Come to think of it; there must be a lot about Alex that I still don't know.

Josiah continues, "Don't you know why he learned to box? Haven't you noticed how no guy has ever asked you out while we were in school? It's not because no one wanted to." Josiah lets out a laugh. "Alex swore that if anyone even laid an eye on you, he would see to it that they could no longer *see*."

"What?" I'm honestly surprised. I mean to think that Alex felt the need to threaten people for me...

"The only reason *I* was able to come anywhere near you is that I've been around long enough to be deemed worthy." Josiah dusts off his shoulders, making a big show out of the fact that Alex likes him.

"Ugh, okay, don't go blowing up that big head of yours about it."

"But he did make it pretty clear that if I *ever* slipped up, that would be it for me. Don't tell him I said this, but..." Josiah shudders. "Alex kind of scares me."

Now, we're both laughing.

I'm laughing so hard tears are springing from my eyes. "I can't believe you're... actually... scared." "If you say a word about this, you're dead." Josiah shakes his fist at me, chuckling.

I can't believe Josiah is scared of Alex.

This is too good.

CHAPTER 29

Athena:

DOWNSTAIRS, MOM IS sitting on the living room couch watching one of my favourite animal documentaries. It's mostly my favourite because Oprah Winfrey does the voice-over. When Oprah narrates, I could listen to her speak all day, every day.

Today's documentary features the Balkan horse breed. I've always wanted to own a horse. When I was younger, I would beg for one nearly every day until Mom said we could compromise by letting me take horseback riding lessons instead. Mom was... a tad bit terrified of horses, so... Dad would take me.

Needless to say, I haven't been back horseback riding since the day he left.

I walk over to the other side of the couch with a bowl of popcorn. "Mind some company?"

"No, I don't mind," Mom says, patting the seat beside me.

It's not that I'm still upset that Mom was talking to Dad without telling us. I just don't understand why. Why she did it, and how she could forgive him.

I guess that's the difference between Mom and me.

I wouldn't have forgiven him.

"Do you remember your third cousin, Sarah?" Mom turns to face me.

"Yeah, she used to come over to the house every once in a while." I remember we instantly clicked on our love for horses. She was only a few years younger than me.

"What about her?" I ask, curious as to why Mom suddenly brought up Sarah.

"She was in an accident. I just got off the phone with her mom not too long ago," Mom says.

"Oh no, that's terrible! Is she okay? What happened?"

I'm on the edge of my seat as Mom describes what happened.

Sarah was volunteering at a horse stable. The owner was so pleased with her that he allowed Sarah to ride the horses for free anytime she wanted. There was a particular horse named Twinkle that she got close to, and the two of them would go horseback riding on the trails around the ranch. One day, the horse was spooked by a garden snake, and Sarah fell off. The horse stepped on Sarah's face while trying to run off, which dislocated her jaw and broke her teeth.

Poor Sarah had to get reconstructive face surgery.

The question Sarah's parents asked her when she got better was, 'will she ever ride a horse again?'

Of course, her parents were terrified throughout the whole thing. It was traumatizing. But when Sarah recovered, she went back to the stable.

There she saw Twinkle, the same horse that had hurt her. Sarah looked up at him, laced her saddle, got on, and cried—and continued to cry. Then, she forgave the horse. She did not punish the horse. Sarah's love for horses was stronger than her pain.

At this point, it is taking every ounce of energy for me not to burst into tears.

I can't believe that she...

Sarah is such a strong girl. I can only imagine the pain and emotional turmoil she has been through.

I look over at my Mom with bloodshot eyes. "I don't—I don't even know what to say."

"Forgiveness doesn't mean that you condone the wrong action." Mom puts a hand on mine. "Forgiveness is to release yourself from the prison you are in. It's to stop the person who hurt you from continuing to hurt you."

Mom is right; holding onto anger only hurts us. It drags on the pain even longer.

My Mom... is the epitome of forgiveness. She is everything that I aspire to be.

She is extraordinary.

The fact that she *chose* to forgive Dad is remarkable. For years, I guess I just thought that she was just... strong?

Superhuman?

When the reality was that she had no choice but to be. Unlike the rest of us, she couldn't exactly afford the luxury to crumple up and cry her eyes out, but that doesn't mean she never wanted to. My Mom picked herself back up the second Dad left, and life moved on because she needed to be strong... for us. Yet, I've never even thanked her for it.

Not once.

I've been too stubborn, too full of myself, to see it. "I'm sorry." My eyes filled with tears as Mom stood up with the bowl of popcorn in her hands. "I'm sorry," I say again.

Mom turns to face me, her brown eyes—the same as mine—searching my face. "For what?"

"For everything." I slowly walk towards her, tears clouding my eyes. "For not making it easy to love me."

Mom's face softens as I continue blabbering. "For not telling you... how much I love you... and how"—I pause, sniffling up my tears—"grateful I am that you stayed. When we all know that there's been plenty of times... and plenty of reasons..."

I let out a weak laugh. "No one would have judged you at all if you ran away. I'm sure you wanted to."

Mom laughs too, gathering me in her arms. "More times than I can count."

CHAPTER 30

Caiden:

I LIE AWAKE IN BED, staring up at the popcorn ceiling. The clock on my nightstand says it is 3:17 a.m., yet I cannot fall asleep, my thoughts keeping me awake. Her words echo in my mind—'I never thought you could be so selfish.' And the undeniable truth was Athena's right.

I am selfish.

Groggy and disoriented, I make my way to the kitchen to grab a glass of water. Before the cup can even reach my lips, it slips from my hand and shatters; thick chunks of glass cascade all over the cold tile floor.

Suddenly my head starts to hurt, and all I can hear is the buzzing in my ears. I press my hands to my ears, trying to block the sound, but it only intensifies and the pain gets worse.

The room is spinning; black dots appear in front of my eyes, and my vision blurs.

Shaking my head, I tell myself to snap out of it, to get it together, but the noise is too loud.

Sinking to the bottom of the floor, I cradle my head in my hands, and the next thing I know, I'm lying crumpled up on the ground.

I lay there, waiting for the feeling to come back into my legs and for the world to stop spinning.

I don't want to feel or think.

About anything.

Instead, I stare at the peeled yellow paint on the edges of the kitchen wall, wondering why I've never noticed it before.

All I want is to be okay.

. . ⁓ . .

The next morning, I wake up with a major headache. My eyes feel heavy, and it hurts to move any part of my face. Clutching the sides of my head, I swallow a few of the pain meds on my dresser, closing my eyes as I wait for the pain to subside.

When it eases up a bit, I head downstairs to see Isabella peacefully eating at the kitchen dining table. Isabella munches on her chocolate crunch cereal, completely content.

I wrap my arms around her shoulders, thinking about the million and one things I have yet to do with her. Isabella squirms, but I refuse to let go. "Hi to you too."

Isabella continues mindlessly munching on her cereal. "I love you, Is," I say, trying not to get choked up.

"Yeah, right back atcha." Isabella looks up at me, probably wondering what is going through my mind. "Is something wrong?"

It's crazy how Isabella can always sense when something is up. She is so much like Mom in that way.

"No, not at all," I say, trying to keep my voice calm and steady. "Just wanted you to know how much I love you, that's all."

"That's great. Now that I know, you can let go now. I'm trying to eat my cereal," Isabella whines.

"No." I hold her tighter, although by now, Isabella is trying to slip out of my grip. "I'm not letting you go," I whisper. "Not now, not *ever*."

Isabella pulls back when she notices the new scar, triangular in shape, on my forearm. "When did you get that?" Isabella asks.

I don't tell her it's from the episode I had last night. Isabella doesn't know I have MS, and I plan to keep it that way.

The last thing I want is for her to worry about me.

Isabella eyes it, an empathetic look on her face. "It must have hurt a lot."

Isabella scurries off, saying she has to get something for me, that I must wait here and not move an inch until she returns.

"Yes, ma'am." I salute her.

Isabella returns with a first aid kit—the one I had gotten for her when she was learning to ride a bike a few years back. "You got this for me because I was always injuring myself when I was learning to bike ride, remember?" Isabella says, opening it up.

"Yeah, I remember."

"But it looks like *you* need it more than me." Isabella holds it out in front of me. "You should keep it."

I meet Isabella's eyes as she points out all the other bruises she sees. "You need to be more careful; we don't want you to seriously injure yourself." Isabella adopts her parent-tone.

I force a laugh. "Yeah, I'm such a klutz. Mom always says I have two left feet."

"Promise you'll be more careful?" Isabella holds out her pinky to make me pinky promise, a thing we always did as kids.

I connect my pinkie with hers, smiling. "Promise."

. . ❧ . .

That afternoon, I see Isabella huddled in a corner with her sketchpad in her hands. Flipping it open, she grabs a pencil and begins to draw. "What are you drawing, Is?"

"A picture," Isabella says like it was stupid of me to even ask that question when the answer was so obvious.

"Oh my gosh, what a revelation. I had no idea. Thanks for clearing that one up for me." That gets her to laugh. "Can I see it?"

"It's not done yet," Isabella says firmly.

So, I sit with her on the floor for about fifteen minutes, waiting ever so patiently—or at least I *try* to.

Isabella looks over at me, groaning, lying on the floor. "What's wrong?" She sounds genuinely concerned that something is wrong with me. "Are you okay?"

"No... the suspense..." I clutch my chest dramatically. "It's killing me."

Isabella sighs a heavy sigh like she is absolutely done with me. "Then just die."

Undeterred, I reach for the picture, but Isabella's got quick reflexes. "Nice try." She moves to the far corner of the room to finish her drawing.

When I try to peek, she turns, shielding the page from my view. I ruffle Isabella's hair, then go upstairs to my room.

• • ⌀ • •

As I strum away on the guitar, my mind flashes back to when Athena was here. Everything reminds me of her, a walk in the park, a song on the radio... Yet still, I feel so conflicted. It's like my body is in fight or flight mode, and I don't know which side I should let win.

I'm torn.

Torn between what I want to do and what I feel is the right thing to do. I can only imagine the horror if the choice I make is the wrong one.

• • ⌀ • •

Deciding I need to get out of the house, I go to sit on the porch. I've been couped up at home for too long.

"Look at you, looking all sorry for yourself." Damon chucks the basketball at me.

Typically, we would play basketball on a beautiful day like today. Honestly, though, I'm not feeling up to it.

"Here to mock me, are you?" I reply, not caring how sad and pathetic I sound.

"No. I'm here because Isabella took pity on your soul and asked me to come."

Great. I'm sure Isabella filled him in on what happened with Athena.

"I'm convinced that you actually *like* to suffer. You've been suffering for so long; you wouldn't even know what to do if you ever felt happy."

I spin the basketball in my hands, needing something else to focus on because day in and day out, all I ever think about is Athena.

"You're making a stupid decision, and yeah, that's coming from me, the *king* of making stupid mistakes," Damon says. "You're only going to regret letting her get away."

Jake steps in; I didn't even notice he had come along too. "The people you care about, that love you—your friends, your Mom, Isabella, and Athena—*No one* can be happy when you're unhappy. So, tell me, *who* exactly are you doing this for? Man, if you are miserable, so are we." Jake takes the ball from me. "All I'm saying is one of us is right, and the other is you."

I look at my friends, the guys I have depended on for the past five years—they were right. I was going about this all wrong.

"But what if it is too late?" I ask them.

Damon punches me in the arm. "It will be if you keep this up. Go after her, man!" "You guys are the best. I'm so lucky to have you as friends," I say, feeling touched.

"Yeah, yeah, we know. Now go!" Jake pushes me.

I will do whatever it takes to win back Athena's heart.

But there's something I need to do first.

CHAPTER 31

Caiden:

OKAY, I NEED A GIRL'S point of view on this. I screwed up, and I desperately need to make it right.

I'll ask Isabella for her advice.

Taking a seat on the edge of Isabella's bed, I put on my best pleading face. "I need your help."

"I'm listening." Isabella stops bouncing up and down on her gymnastic ball.

"Okay, so I messed up my chance with Athena. How do I get her back?"

Isabella taps her chin, contemplating. "Depends... how badly did you mess up?"

"Well..."

"*That* bad, huh?" Isabella nods. "Well, then, there's only one thing you can do. Keep apologizing and shower her with gifts. It'll take some time for her to forgive you."

"Thanks, Is!" I plant a kiss on her cheek.

"Ew, gross." Isabella swats me away.

• • ⚬✿⚬ • •

With help from Sky, we work on what I like to call 'Operation X.' Okay, so the name needs a little work, but it's kind of growing on me now. I like it.

We are, well, *I* am, trying to be as quiet as a mouse because the last thing I want to do is wake Athena up.

It is close to 11 p.m., and we are sneaking into Athena's bedroom to drop off the gifts I made her. Sky, on the other hand, *isn't* being very quiet.

"Could you be a little louder?" I say, my voice dripping with sarcasm. "I'm not sure it will wake Athena up."

"Relax," Sky says, sensing my sarcasm. "If anyone knows the consequences of angering the sleeping beast, it would be *me*, so don't sweat it."

We carefully place the ceramic bear, pig, and elephant I made in different spots in Athena's bedroom.

Now, we wait.

Sky will let me know how the plan goes, as in whether or not Athena is ready to forgive me.

I'm *really* hoping she does.

CHAPTER 32
Athena:

AS SOON AS I OPEN MY eyes, I sense something is off. Why does it feel as if someone was in my room?

Blinking the sleep from my eyes, I notice that there is a...

Wait, what is that?

I walk over to my navy dresser, picking up what looks like glass or maybe a ceramic bear with a sticky note attached to its round belly. 'I'm beary sorry, please forgive me.'

What in the world...

Then, on my wooden bookshelf in the corner of my room, I find another one. This time it's a cute little pig. The attached note reads: 'Are you...'

My gaze settles on the grey elephant beside my wardrobe, which has yet another sticky note. 'Still ->' The arrow beside the message points to my closet door.

I open it, not sure what I expect to be inside, when I see that the wall inside my closet is filled, and I mean *filled,* with sticky notes, spelling out the words, 'mad at me? Please don't be. I'm such an idiot. I'm sorry. —Caiden'

He even shaped the sticky notes into a pink heart in the background, with the yellow sticky notes on top spelling out the words.

Okay, that is adorably cute.

When I go into the bathroom, I find even *more* sticky notes all over the mirror.

There is a smiley face sticky note sitting in the middle of the mirror. Beside it is a pink sticky note that reads, 'put this sticky note on the outside of your bedroom door if you are ready to forgive me.'

As much as I wanted to... I just couldn't bring myself to do it.

I couldn't leave the sticky note on the outside of my door. It's not because I can't forgive him.

I *do*.

All of a sudden, I felt scared.

Scared of letting my walls down... Letting someone in again means I have to be vulnerable, and just thinking about that scares me.

Caiden:

SKY MESSAGES ME USING the walkie-talkie she got for us. She insisted that if we were going to team up for this mission, we do it right.

That girl's got spunk.

She is also really bossy and kind of scares me, so I make sure to listen to what she says.

"Abort mission!" Sky speaks into the walkie. "Operation X is a no-go. I repeat, abort."

"Roger that." I slowly climb down from the tree I was sitting in, right outside Athena's bedroom window. "Time for Plan B."

Okay, so that plan didn't *exactly* go as I wanted, but it's okay. I came prepared. It is now time for Plan B. Hopefully, Athena will see how genuinely sorry I am and forgive me.

I just have to be patient.

And wait.

Two things that I am not so great at, but for her, it will all be worth it.

Athena:

I CAN HEAR SKY TALKING to Violet downstairs, warning her about coming up here. Sky is so loud that I can hear her from up in my room.

"Disclaimer, she's a little..." Sky trails off.

Arms crossed, I'm the least bit impressed that Sky is overreacting. "What?" I yell from upstairs. "Go on, continue. What *am* I?"

"Snappy." Sky fills in the blank.

Violet knocks on my door before slowly walking in. "Hey Hun, how are we doing in here?"

"Fine. Great. Fantastic." I reply while continuing to stuff my face with M&M's.

My mind has been spiraling out of control, my emotions going from sad and gloomy to angry and wanting to punch a hole through the wall. I just don't know what to do or how to feel. I am mad at myself for not being able to make up my mind about all this...

Alex

Dad

Caiden

"Ook. We're just going to take that away." Violet starts to slide the bowl away from me, but when I growl in protest, she lets go.

Don't judge me, okay?

When I am stressed, I eat, and by eat, I mean I devour anything that has sugar in it, hoping the sugar high will help me feel better—even if only temporarily.

"Feisty today, are we?" Violet sits on my bed. "Do you know what you need? To blow off some steam."

170

I'm not really in the mood to go anywhere. Right now, all I want to do is curl up in my bed and sleep the day away.

"Come on, let's go. I'm taking you out of this room, even if I have to drag you out. This pity party is over. You have been holed up here for three days. It's time to get up."

Violet opens the blinds that have been closed for the past few days. The sun is too bright; it stings my eyes.

"Ah, it burns!" I cover my eyes, shielding them from the sun's rays.

Violet pushes me into the shower, telling me I stink, and she is staying here until I come out dressed and ready to go.

. . ໖. . .

Violet takes me go-karting. As much fun as that usually would be for me, my heart just isn't in it today.

We spend a few hours on the racetrack, Violet's score crushing mine by a landslide. At the last race, I swear she took pity on me and let me win because I doubt she actually couldn't recover when I knocked her car into the ditch.

Normally, Violet would bounce back, faster and harder, and show me who I'm messing with.

I was grateful for the distraction.

I really needed to get out of the house.

. . ໖. . .

On the car ride home, I get a text from Caiden.

Caiden: You're shutting me out. Maybe not because you want to, but because it's the easy way out.

I sigh, reading the text message, knowing that Caiden is right.

Once again, I'm running away.

Like a coward.

I receive another text message; this one is from Mom.

Mom: Caiden's in the backyard waiting for you. He's refusing to leave until he gets to see you.

I shake my head, thinking that this guy is really something.

Caiden just doesn't give up, does he?

· · ᔕᵒᔕ · ·

Back at home, my heart is racing as I slide open the kitchen patio door to meet Caiden. He is sitting in the backyard under the oak tree on the wooden swing.

I study Caiden for a moment; he looks anxious. He's muttering to himself, but I can't quite make out what he is saying.

Caiden jumps when I tap him on the shoulder, but as soon as he sees it's me, a smile lights up his face. "Hi," he says, taking my hands into his.

"Let's set the record straight," I say, trying to keep my voice even and steady. "I was right, and you were wrong." Caiden continues smiling, looking at me with earnest sincerity in his eyes.

"Fine, I'll let you be right just this *once*. I'm sorry I'm such an idiot."

"Hmph. As long as you know."

He kisses my nose, my cheek, and finally, my lips. His arms swiftly swoop around me, pulling me closer to him.

It sends little happy flutters in my stomach.

I love nothing more in this world than being right here—in his arms.

I wrap my arms around him. "No, I'm the one who should be apologizing." Shaking my head, I say, my voice serious, "I'm sorry for all the terrible things I said to you. You're not selfish. I didn't mean it. Can you forgive me?"

"You're forgiven." Smiling, he wraps his arms tighter around me.

"You. are. Crushing. My. Spleen."

"You don't even know *where* your spleen is." I swat him on the back, and Caiden throws his head back, laughing.

CHAPTER 33
Athena:

TODAY IS A SPECIAL day, and I need an outfit that fits the occasion.

I rummage through my closet in search of something decent to wear. Something that looks good, but not like I'm trying *too* hard to look good, you know?

Sky has an eye for fashion. She is the perfect person for me to ask for help with this.

"Sky!" I yell from the top of the stairs.

"What?"

"Come!"

"Why?"

Why does she have to ask so many questions?

"Just come, and you'll find out!"

"Ugh!" Sky drags her feet when she comes in. "What do you want?"

I smile sweetly at her. "I need help."

"Duh, that's nothing new. You're *now* figuring that out?"

Well then, that's not very nice, but whatever. "With picking out an outfit."

That got Sky's attention. Now she is all ears. "Ooo, what's the occasion?

All giddy and excited, I tell Sky that I need the perfect outfit for my first date with Caiden tonight.

"Move. I already have the perfect outfit in mind." Sky shoves me to the side as she scans through the clothes in my closet.

"Hmm..." She contemplates, tapping her chin.

Sky holds up a lace-off-the-shoulder cream chiffon dress. "Nope, that's way too much."

"Fine."

Sky searches for another option, and her gaze lands on the burgundy sweater dress. "*This* is the one."

Not really my style anymore. I haven't worn that in ages.

"I don't think so," I say, shaking my head.

Sky takes a deep breath. "Okay, what about this? This colour would look great on you." She's holding up a jade green jumpsuit.

I make a face. "Yeah, no."

Sky throws her hands up in the air. "You know what? You're going to have to figure this out yourself. I'm done." She walks out of my bedroom, shaking her head.

Wait, the date is only an hour away. I need Sky's help.

"Wait! Don't go. I need your help!"

"Yeah, well, I'm *trying* to help you, and you keep shutting down all my suggestions. So clearly, you don't want it."

I grab onto her shirt sleeve, begging her. "I'm sorry, please!!"

Sky groans, annoyed. "Ugh, why are you so needy?"

In the end, I take Sky's advice and go with her second pick, the burgundy sweater dress.

· · ❧ · ·

Today is our first day—our first official day as a couple.

Mom and Collin stand by the front door, giddy as they take a picture of the two of us. I'm smiling so much my cheeks burn.

Caiden set up a beautiful rooftop date for us, a date under the stars.

This is going to be the *best* date ever.

Climbing up the ladder leaning at the side of the house, I notice Caiden is still standing at the bottom, staring at his phone. "You coming?" I call out to him from the top of the ladder.

"Why are you smiling so much?" he asks, making his way up the ladder.

We sit on the fluffy blankets and pillows spread out on the roof. "Look." He passes his phone to show me. "Your smile almost takes up half your face... your eyes are little slits." He's laughing at me, as usual.

"Oh, shut up. I look great."

"You look beautiful."

"Thanks, you don't look half-bad yourself," I say, snatching one of the French macaroons that Caiden brought for us, along with a hot steaming thermos filled with hot chocolate.

Caiden puts a hand to his chest, mock offended. "Half bad? I am the bomb."

"You wish. If anything, I am." I take a sip from my thermos; it's delicious. The hot chocolate has a rich, creamy, decadent taste.

Looking up at the night sky filled with stars, I think how incredible it is that every day we can enjoy the infinite beauty of the charcoal sky glittered with stars that light up the night.

Caiden rolls over to face me, his head propped up by his elbows. "What is your dream? What do you wish for?"

"Honestly? I'm not sure. I mean, as a kid, I thought I had it all figured out... or at least had an *idea* of what I wanted... but now..." I pause to look up at him under the fridge of my lashes. "I feel so lost... like I don't even know who I am anymore or what I want."

Caiden patiently waits as I let it all out.

"That sounds stupid, I know..." Now that I'm saying the words out loud, I see how ludicrous it sounds. "I'm all of 19, and I *still* don't have my life figured out."

It's pretty pathetic.

"No, it's not stupid at all." His voice is genuine and sincere. "*No one's* life is exactly as we pictured it to be... I feel like we hold ourselves to such unrealistically high standards, only to punish ourselves for *not* being able to reach them. *Of course*, we can't reach them since they were unattainable in the first place." Caiden smiles. "So, don't be so hard on yourself."

"You're doing it again."

Caiden wrinkles his brow. "Doing what?" He takes a bite of the salted caramel macaroon.

"It's almost as if you can read my mind." Shaking my head, I think it's almost unbelievable how he does this every time. "How do you do that? Are you just superb at guessing, or do you know me that well?"

"My Spidey-senses told me."

"Oh, brother."

Lying here next to him under the night sky, I think that at this moment, everything is exactly as I want it to be, and I feel... *happy*.

"What do you wish for?"

Caiden pulls at a loose thread from one of the blankets, examining it. "I just want... the people I love to be happy." I stare at him, completely gob-smacked.

"Um, why are you looking at me like that?"

"You are... the most selfless human being that I know."

He's quick to object, being the humble guy that he is. "No, *far* from it."

"No, I mean it." Smiling, I meet his gaze. "I wish you could see yourself the way that I see you. You are *inspiring*."

A look passes on Caiden's face; he seems more distant, aloof. "Hey." I touch his shoulder. "Is something wrong?"

"No, why?" He smiles, but the light is gone from his eyes. Something seems... off.

Then, like a switch, Caiden is back laughing and goofing around a few seconds later.

Maybe it's nothing. Maybe it's just me overthinking things as usual. Even still...

Caiden holds his hands out in front of me like he is going to tickle me. He better not.

As he inches closer, a slow smile spreads across Caiden's face. "Don't," I warn, sliding away from him.

"Tickle me, and I won't be responsible for the consequences." I give him what I hope looks like a menacing stare.

A devious smile plays on his lips as he wraps his arms around me instead.

Caiden holds me close in the biggest, sweetest teddy bear hug, and I melt into his touch. He drops his head down to my shoulder and lets out a long sigh. After a little while, his fingers move gently up and down my arms. I don't want to let go of him. I just want to sit here. With him. So close that there is no space between us.

Alex bangs on my bedroom window, startling us, then pushes it open. He glares at Caiden, giving him an 'I've got my eyes on you' stare. "No funny business. I'll sit right here so I can see you. What are your intentions tonight?"

Okay, that's enough.

"Do you want to die? Do you have a death wish? Come here." I reach for his ear, and Alex quickly closes the window, running away.

CHAPTER 34
Caiden:

"COME HERE, GIRL." I bend down to rub Luna on the belly. She rolls over, as happy as can be.

Today, we are taking Luna to the dog groomers for a well-needed haircut. Her fur has grown out so long that it almost covers her *eyes*.

It's adorable, but I'm sure she would much rather like to see clearly.

Athena said she wanted to come along, and she would have my *head* if I went without her.

She loves Luna as much as I do, which is one of the many things I love about her.

Slipping my phone into my back pocket, I'm ready to head out the door, picking up Luna's bag for the groomers I left by the front door. My phone buzzes with an incoming text from Athena.

I'm expecting that the text will say she is on her way, but I am surprised to see that it's a text from Violet from Athena's phone. Athena's having a bit of a meltdown. I don't think she will be able to make it to the groomers today.

I quickly type back, What? I'm heading over to her place now.

Mom tells me not to worry about it; she will take Luna to the groomers. "Thanks, Mom," I say before marching over to Athena's house. I soon break into a run.

· · ❧ · ·

"Where is she?" I ask, still out of breath.

Violet lets me in and tells me to sit on the couch. "We should give her some time to calm down," she says calmly.

178

Okay, give her time.

Yeah, no problem at all.

I can do that.

We sit for about 20 minutes, Josiah pacing up and down and Violet nervously looking up the stairs, wondering if Athena is okay.

Josiah's pacing is only making me freak out *even* more.

"That's it. I'm going to go check on her," Josiah says, but I stop him by putting a hand on his shoulder.

"No, I'll go." I get up from the couch, making my way up the stairs as Josiah calls out after me.

"Her room is—"

"I know," I say, taking two steps at a time when I hear a loud bang.

"How... How does he know that? Has *he* been in her room?" I hear Josiah ask, demanding answers. Violet sits him back down. "Relax."

· · ᕱᕱ · ·

Upstairs, I knock on Athena's door, noting that it's become oddly quiet. Is this the calm before the storm?

"Is it safe to come in?" I slowly open the door; I barely have my foot in before I have to duck to avoid the flying object sailing toward my head.

"Okay." I slide into the room, backing into the corner. "Remind me not to let you anywhere near a gun. You have scarily good aim."

Athena's ripping a box apart, shredding it to pieces. She flings paint and paintbrushes in my direction, telling me to get lost.

"Go... go away!" Athena yells as she continues throwing, but I don't budge, so she shoves me.

"Please... just leave." She's slamming her fists into my chest, begging me to go, tears brimming her eyes.

"No." I catch her fists in my hands, forcing her to look up at me. "I'm not leaving you. It's fine, take it all out on me, but I'm here to stay."

I move my hands up to her face to still her staggered breathing. "Hey, hey, it's okay. Look at me, take a deep breath."

She closes her eyes and takes a deep breath. "Am I an object that can be tossed aside and picked back up when he changes his mind? Does he think he can just buy me off?" She motions to the opened box on the floor containing the paint supplies that must be from her dad.

"Did he think I'd just sit around pining for him after *all* these years?" Her voice cracks as she continues, "I'm not an object... I'm—I'm a human being... and I deserve... more than that."

It breaks my heart to see her like this, and I wish I could take all the pain away.

"Of course you do." I hold her gaze. "You deserve the world." Athena's face crumples as she sobs, her cries primitive and raw.

I wrap my arms around her shoulders, pulling her into a hug. "I'm sorry," Athena says, her voice muffled by her tears.

"Don't be. It's okay. Let it all out."

"But I'm getting snot all over your shirt."

"Good. I never liked this shirt anyway," I say, which makes her laugh through her tears. "Want to go for a walk?"

"Okay."

• • ⁓ • •

Hand in hand, we walk down the sidewalk to the Scoops o' Joy Ice cream Parlor.

Athena picked the Bunny Tracks double scoop ice cream on a waffle cone, and I got the Jamoca Almond Fudge ice cream sundae with cherries and whipped cream.

We sit on a wooden bench nearby as we nibble away on our ice cream in silence. I try to crack a few jokes here and there, but I can tell that Athena's mind is somewhere else.

Gently, I nudge her in the arm, offering her a warm smile. "I'm sorry my sour face is spoiling our date," Athena says, looking down at the ice cream in her hands.

"Date?" I tease her, hoping that she will at least crack a tiny smile. "Who says this was a date?"

It doesn't work, though.

Clearing my throat, I mention what I hope will put her mind at ease. "You don't have to say anything if you don't want to. We can just sit here and eat ice cream, or... if you feel like talking, that's okay too."

"Okay..." Athena takes a few minutes to collect her thoughts first. Then she begins to tell me everything that's happened with her dad so far and how upset she's feeling about everything.

"I'm sorry you had to go through all of that," I say, meeting her eyes.

"It's okay." She sighs, continuing to take a few licks of her ice cream.

I spoon another bite of the sundae into my mouth, letting it melt. "Of course, I wasn't there, and I can only imagine the pain you are feeling right now and... whether or not you decide to forgive him is entirely your choice." I take her hand in mine, watching her face intently. "More than anything else, I want you to be happy. But can you truly be happy if you don't forgive him?"

Athena meets my eyes for a moment, and then her eyes land on the family sitting on the bench across from us. "My dad was my whole universe," she says, her voice wobbling. "When he left... it was like my world came crashing down, and it took years for me to *barely* manage to pick up the pieces."

Athena looks over at me, sadness clouding her features. "I'm not sure I'm ready to let him in again... or maybe I'm just being overly sensitive about the whole thing."

My finger hooks under her chin, tilting her face to mine. "Can I tell you what I think?"

She nods. "You have a strong sense of loyalty to your friends and family, and that's why you're very hurt when they let you down. You give out love and rightfully expect the same love in return. But that's not because you are sensitive; you have a *big* heart, so when you love someone, you give them *all* of you, and it hurts if they don't do the same."

Athena smiles with the warmest light in her eyes. "That is the kindest thing anyone has ever said to me."

I grin, happy to see her smiling again. "Well, you should hear kind things more often."

CHAPTER 35

Athena:

WE HAVE PLANS TO SEE the new movie that just came out today. It's a musical, of course, Caiden's *favourite*. I don't mind musicals, but I can't say they are my cup of tea.

Caiden, of course, only sees that as a challenge He is bent on getting me to change my mind about them. This musical, he says, will be the one that makes me fall in love with musicals.

This shall be interesting.

Before I start the car, I fish my phone out of my pocket to send Caiden a quick text telling him I am on my way over.

That's weird.

Mom called me three times.

My phone must have been on silent again; I didn't even hear it ring. She sent me a text too.

Alex got injured at the gym. We are at the hospital with him now.

That doesn't sound good.

He's been hurt countless times before, but not once has he gone to the hospital for injuries. So, for Alex to be at the hospital, it must be a pretty serious injury.

I hope he doesn't end up needing surgery.

I call Caiden apologizing, saying that we are going to have to reschedule and see the movie at a later date. He's understanding about the whole thing and tells me not to worry. "Go be with Alex. It's okay. Let me know how it goes."

I hang up the phone, heading over to the hospital. It's not far from our house, only a 35-minute drive, 45 if there is traffic.

At the hospital, the doctor tells us that Alex has a hairline fracture. His arm needs a cast, and he will need to wear a sling while it heals. It will take 6 to 8 weeks to heal completely, so it will be necessary for Alex to modify his activities during that time.

This *also* means no more boxing for a while. I bet Alex isn't too happy about that.

Alex is glued to his phone, watching the Raptors basketball game. He looks completely relaxed and content, almost as if he's back at home watching TV on the living room couch when in actuality, he's here at Mount Pleasant Hospital with a hairline fracture in his arm.

Alex seems okay... but why do I have this nagging feeling that Alex is only showing us what he *wants* us to see?

Like, maybe underneath that chill, laid-back exterior, there is a whole other layer?

"Thank you, Dr. Perrin," Mom says, pulling out her phone to call Collin. He couldn't get out of work. Collin was on a call with his manager when we called him.

"Yes, he's going to be just fine," Mom says, talking to Collin on the phone. "Of course, it's Alex. He's always okay."

Alex murmurs, turning his head towards us from the hospital bed. "Why does everyone always assume that I'm okay?"

Mom tells Collin she will call him back. "What's wrong Alex? Is it throbbing? I'll go call the doctor to up the meds." Mom scurries off to find Dr. Perrin, leaving me in the room with Alex.

"I'm not okay!" It's as if something inside Alex snaps. "I'm not..." His chin trembles; it looks like he is about to cry.

In my entire life, I have never seen my brother cry.

"I'm not okay..." Eyes bloodshot red, Alex looks up at me, and it just tears me in half. "Dad left me too."

I was selfish, thinking I was the only one in pain.

Pulling up the chair to sit beside him, I rest my hand on his shoulder. "I'm sorry."

Alex sniffles, trying to hold back his tears.

"You were having a hard time too..." I paused to wipe my tears with the back of my hand. "I'm sorry I didn't pay enough attention to how you were feeling."

The thing about broken hearts is, unlike a broken bone, it doesn't get the time and attention it needs to heal. It goes undetected by the naked eye, so no one really knows the pain you are feeling on the inside.

. . ◦◈◦ . .

That night, had Caiden stopped by, worried sick about Alex. When I arrive home, he's sound asleep on the living room couch.

He's going to wake up in the middle of the night. It's freezing cold down here.

I run upstairs to grab a nice thick blanket and a pillow to put under his head. I sit with him for a bit before heading upstairs to bed.

Around midnight, I am drawn downstairs by the sound of someone whimpering.

Is someone... crying?

I check on Sky and Rain, but they are fast asleep in their bedrooms. Alex is sleeping, too. If everyone is sleeping, where is the sound coming from?

I tiptoe down the stairs to where Caiden is on the couch, sleeping. "Please..." Caiden says, shaking his head.

I reach for his hand. "Caiden, what's wrong?"

"Please... don't leave me..." He's breaking out in a cold sweat. "I'm sorry... I'm sorry," Caiden whimpers as tears roll from his hazel eyes.

Cradling him in my arms, I rock him softly. "Hey, hey... It's okay," I say, tears filling my own eyes.

"Please don't leave," he pleads.

Stroking his hair, I assure him that is *never* going to happen. "Don't worry, I'm right here, and I'm not going anywhere," I say, rubbing his back in circles like my Mom used to do for me when I was little and had had a bad dream.

"I'm sorry." He wraps his arms around me, tightening his grip.

"It's okay, it'll be okay," I say soothingly, hoping it will be.

. . ✂ . .

I awake to find my favorite pair of hazel eyes staring right back at me. Startled, I rush to get up, smoothing my unruly curly hair as I jump off the brown leather couch.

I risk a glance at myself in the hall mirror, only adding to my discomfort and dismay when I see how completely disheveled I look.

Please tell me it was all a dream, and very soon I'll wake up from this terrible nightmare.

"Um... I got to..." Struggling to form a coherent sentence, I blurt out, "I got to go... iron my cat."

"You're what?" I can hear the laughter in Caiden's voice before I run upstairs to the bathroom.

Finally, I can breathe.

I can't believe I *actually* fell asleep. Nice one, Athena. Great job.

Brushing my teeth, I allow my mind to wander back to last night, Caiden's nightmare. He sounded so... scared. How long has he been suffering from nightmares? Was that the reason he said he couldn't sleep?

. . ✂ . .

My nose follows the smell of food, something buttery and sweet, leading me back downstairs to the kitchen. It's Collin. He's cooking up a storm... with Caiden.

"Morning, baby girl, can you set the table for us? The food is just about done," Collin says, flipping the thick fluffy pancake on the stove.

"Sure." I walk over to the other side of the kitchen, opening the cream-colored wooden cupboard to get the white ceramic dishes we use *strictly* for when company is over.

Reaching up to the top shelf, I'm careful not to lose my balance because if I broke these, I would be dead.

Mom has an obsession with silverware and cutlery.

I have butterfingers, so it would not take much for these dishes to fall out of my hands. Of course, Caiden has to take this very moment to poke me in my ribcage.

I somehow regain my balance so that the dishes do not topple over.

"Caiden!" I roll my eyes at him, and his face breaks into a smile.

He can be so childish at times.

We all sit around the kitchen table and have breakfast together. This is nice. I think I could actually get used to this.

Alex pours syrup on his mountain of pancakes. "Are you sure you want to date her?"

I can see Alex is back to his regular annoying self. He must have recovered pretty quickly from his injury.

"Of course," Caiden says.

"I mean..." Alex trails off. "She's kind of *a lot*."

Thanks for the vote of confidence, Alex. I really appreciate it.

"I'd rethink that one if I were you," Alex adds.

Rain turns her attention to Caiden. "Want to see this photo album I made?"

Rain better not be doing what I think she is doing.

"Sure." Caiden smiles at her.

The sparkle in her mischievous eyes tells me that my guess was correct.

Rain slides over in her chair. "It's an album of Athena's most embarrassing moments."

Caiden raises an eyebrow. "Oh, this, I gotta see."

Eyes wide, I'm screaming internally.

This can't be happening.

As Rain scrolls through the photos, Caiden takes a sip from his drink, trying to hide his smile.

Kill me now and save me from my misery.

"Hey Rain, remember that time you wanted to borrow my teal sweater?" I was resorting to bribery. I know, the lowest of the low.

Rain's voice fell flat. "Yeah, you said no."

Clearly, she has every intention of making me beg.

"I know," I say, trying to keep my voice as polite as ever when, really, I want to strangle her. "Well, I take it back. You can borrow it."

"Thanks," Rains says simply. The two of them laughed, pointing at the phone screen.

I let out a breath. "Caiden."

"Hmm?"

"Remember that *thing* we had to go to? Don't wanna be late," I lie, trying to rush this along.

"What thing?" Caiden's only half-listening. He's too busy telling Rain to forward those horrid pictures to him.

He even saves the photo of me devouring a plate of chicken wings as his screensaver.

Sky sits forward in her seat across from us, her eyes gleaming. "You know... *I* take bribes."

"Not now, Sky."

I don't have the time or the energy to deal with her mind games right now.

"Oh really? Okay then, I'll just tell Caiden about the time you pranced into my room in desperate need of my advice."

I can practically see the wheels turning in Sky's calculative little head.

"Oh, Caiden—" Sky says before I clamp my hand over her mouth.

What an opportunist.

"How many of these do you have?" Caiden asks Rain, sounding genuinely impressed.

"Don't." I mouth to Caiden, who shrugs with pretend confusion in return. "What?" He asks, all innocently.

Caiden:

THAT WAS BY FAR THE *funniest* thing I have ever witnessed in my entire life.

Athena looks relieved to finally be out of there. She was itching to leave the *second* Rain pulled out her phone, but it was too good of an opportunity to pass up. I couldn't just go. "Your family is truly one of a kind. They are so much fun to be around. Can I move in?"

"Fun? That's debatable. You only say that because you don't have to live with them." Athena smirks. "Trust me. If anyone spent a day in my house, they wouldn't even *last* the day."

I beg to differ; it can't be that bad. Plus, I never grew up with a big family. I'd love to see what that feels like. "I'm up for the challenge."

Athena pokes me. "You were enjoying every minute of it, weren't you?"

I laugh, looking at my new screen saver, then back at her. "Loosen up a little." Athena stops walking and turns to me with a serious look on her face.

"So, umm... do you..." Athena takes a deep breath, and when she speaks, I can hear the nerves lacing her words. "Want to talk about it?"

I wonder why she looks so nervous suddenly. I slip my hand into hers. "About what?"

"Last night..." Athena pauses for a few seconds, her eyes meeting mine. "The nightmare... you looked so scared."

I smile, but I'm sure she can tell it's forced. "It's nothing."

I wish she didn't have to see me like that. I don't want her to worry about me.

Athena shakes her head. "No, Caiden, it's not nothing. Something is obviously bothering you."

"It's fine." I insist, placing my free hand on her arm. "I can handle it."

She stares at me, not saying anything for a while. "But what if..." Athena looks up at me, her voice soft. "You can't? You don't have to handle it all on your own."

No, it just wouldn't be fair.

I don't want to lessen my burden by throwing it at someone else.

"It's really sweet of you to want to help, but I've got to deal with this one on my own, okay?" I kiss Athena's hand, staring into her eyes with another tight-lipped smile.

We go for a walk. Since it is such a gorgeous day out, it'd feel like such a waste not to. On our stroll, we pass by a family with boy and girl twins.

Athena stops to wave at the little girl in pigtails, asking her name. "Hey, there. What's your name, gorgeous?"

"Gabriella," she says, smiling at Athena.

Athena's face is glowing as she talks to Gabriella and her brother Nate, asking the parents how old they are.

Something about it makes my stomach sink to the floor.

I'm trying really hard not to think about it, but I can't stop my mind from wondering.

All I can think about is how much Athena will miss out on being with me. Life with me will be... exhausting and frustrating. Not only do I have all this emotional baggage with myself and with my dad, my MS only makes things more difficult.

Soon, I'll be confined to a wheelchair and unable to groom or do anything for myself anymore. My body will start to shut down. It would be nearly impossible for us to have kids...

I can't—

I can't give Athena what she wants.

I don't want her to sacrifice her dream of becoming a mother for me.

"Maybe we should..." I say, forcing myself to say the words out loud. "Take a break."

"What?"

"Maybe... I should take some time to think."

The hurt flashed just for the briefest moment across her face but was replaced by understanding and concern. "Okay." She looks up at me, searching my face. "If that's what you want... I will respect your decision."

. . ⚬⫯⚬ . .

As I walk Athena back home, it is painstakingly silent between us the entire way there. I feel *really* guilty about springing this break-up on Athena. Especially since we just started going out. It has been less than a month since we started dating, and here I go ruining everything before it even had a chance to start.

Being with Athena has been a dream come true. I love every minute we share, and yet...

I can't stop this nagging voice in my head that tells me that as much as I want to be...

I'm not good enough for her.

As we reach Athena's front door, she hesitates before heading inside. She pulls me into a tight hug instead. "I'm here for you if you ever want someone to talk to, okay?"

My heart drops to the floor, the guilt eating away at me.

I manage a slight nod, unable to bring myself to say how I'm really feeling.

I bite the inside of my cheek to stop myself from changing my mind.

This was the right thing to do.

. . ⚬⫯⚬ . .

Back at the house, I kick off my shoes at the door. Good job, Caiden. You made the right choice. This break was for the best. It'll give her a chance to realize that this relationship was a huge mistake.

Maybe now is the best time to make a clean break once and for all.

After all, who could ever want to be with me? Bruises and all?

I'm not confident in myself or my ability to give her all of me, to shed light on the parts that even I don't want to see. It's ugly and scary. I don't... I don't know if I could be the man she wants me to be. I just fear that I'll only fail miserably. I'm not worthy of her. I don't deserve her; she deserves *so* much more.

Athena is a ray of light that shines in the dark. She is compassionate and kind, and there is a softness in her eyes. Athena should be valued and cherished, and I... don't have anything to offer her.

I'm afraid I'm not the right match for her.

CHAPTER 36

Athena:

I WANT TO PUT MYSELF in Caiden's shoes to understand how he might be feeling right now.

Things had been going great, at least I *hoped* they had been, and then Caiden said he needed a break. Understandably, he must have a lot on his mind, and I'm not upset with him or anything.

I just... feel guilty that I couldn't do more for him, be *there* for him.

I can't help but feel bothered by the fact that there is so much I don't know about him.

So, I decided to do some research. I take out my laptop and search for as much information as possible on young men with MS.

The words that jumped out at me are...

Low-Self Esteem
Feelings of Inadequacy
Vulnerability
Hopelessness
Fear
Anxiety

Quite a few men who experience living with this disease have commented that it takes a certain type of strength for a man to be open about his feelings and MS symptoms.

One person said, 'We men don't like to show weakness, but what I have learned is that it takes more strength to show weakness than to hide it.'

Wow... I had no idea. I feel terrible for not noticing all along.

Caiden must have felt so alone, unable to voice how he feels.

I think a lot of unnecessary pressure is put on men to be strong—to be a *man*.

Men don't cry. Men don't break down, or they will be seen as weak. But that's such an unfair expectation to have in the first place because, like women, men have feelings, too, and they shouldn't have to feel ashamed of it.

The article goes on to say that 'many of us feel we will only hold people back and become a hindrance in their lives, so we distance ourselves to save them from being unhappy.'

Could that be true?

Could it be that Caiden is worried that he will be unable to make *me* happy?

But that's so far from the truth.

I think it's time I let Caiden know how much he means to me.

I know exactly what I am going to do.

CHAPTER 37

Athena:

THIS IS IT.

This is the end of my life; *this* is how I will die.

It's too bad, really. I'd much rather go out with a bang. But no, I realize sadly that this will be the end of my life.

"Come on! You're holding us back. Let's go!" Violet yells from a few feet away, her head partially covered by the huge sycamore trees.

The hot afternoon sun beats down on me, drying out every last bit of my energy. "No, go on without me." I'm panting and out of breath.

Although I can't see her face clearly from here, I'm pretty sure Violet is rolling her eyes all the way to the back of her head.

I don't know how much longer I can do this.

Exactly *why* are we doing this?

I sprawl out on the hard-packed grass, not having the strength or the motivation to go any further. "Just leave me here to die."

Violet treads backward and peels me off the ground, pulling me up to my feet. "You are clearly out of shape," she says.

"Ugh, do I have to?" I plead, wanting nothing more than to end this misery.

Violet laughs manically. "This was *your* idea, remember? You were the one that wanted to go on this hike. Not me, *you*. So, you, of all people, don't get to back out now."

Okay, so maybe... I might have suggested the idea. But that's only because I was willing to do anything to keep my mind off Caiden.

He hasn't responded to any of my messages, and Violet threatened to confiscate my phone if I text him again.

So, here we are on this hike as a distraction.

Either way, I'm still not impressed to be here. "I really hate you sometimes."

"The feeling is mutual."

"You know what? This is your fault, too, for listening to me."

"Oh, yeah?"

"I mean, neither of us has any sense of direction. So, it's not a matter of *if* we get lost, but *when*. The two of us should not be left alone unattended." I gesture to the empty space around us. "Now there's no one to save us. That was the first mistake."

"So here we are, stranded on this hike with no idea how to get back to the car. You know—" Violet seems to lose her train of thought, glancing down at her phone.

"You were saying something?"

Violet looks distracted, a goofy smile on her face. "Huh? Oh, nothing."

"Who were you texting?"

"Hmm? Oh, my mom."

"Uh-huh." Yeah, there's no way it's her mom.

Judging from the look on her face, she must be texting a guy. It's okay. Since I dragged her on this hike, I owe her one, so I won't harass her.

I'll wait for her to tell me.

• • ✺ • •

When I get home, I take a long hot shower, then collapse onto my bed feeling sore and tired.

Every inch of my body hurts.

I haven't had a solid full-body workout in quite a while.

My stomach grumbles ferociously. It's almost 7 p.m., and I haven't eaten dinner yet. I wonder if Violet is up for going out to eat Thai food tonight.

After that dreadful hike, I owe her *big* time. It'll be my treat.

Yeah, that's an excellent idea.

I throw on some sweats and head over to Violet's place. We can chill out, watch a movie for a bit, and then I can get dressed for dinner when I'm there.

· · ✧ · ·

Without bothering to knock, I turn the knob on Violet's bedroom door. "Hey, can I borrow—"

"Hey, A, what—what are you doing here?"

"Why are you so jumpy? I want to treat you to dinner tonight. I came to grab the floral dress I left here." I make to open Violet's closet door, but she throws herself in front of it.

"Um... why are you stopping me from going in there? Are you hiding something?"

"No, it's just messy, that's all."

"Seriously? You've seen what a mess mine is; it's fine."

Violet puts her arms in front of the closet door, still trying to block me. "Geesh, it's not like you are hiding a dead body in there," I say, shaking my head.

I freeze when Violet doesn't answer. "You're *not* hiding a dead body in there, are you?"

"You promised you would help me."

"Yeah, I promised, hoping it would never have to come to that." Laughing, I say, "Please tell me this is just another one of your sick, twisted idea of a joke."

Violet and I had made this pact that if it ever came down to it, we would even help each other dispose of a body. But I mean, it was a *joke*. We weren't being serious.

Or at least, that's what I thought.

"Well—" Violet opens her mouth to say something, then snaps it shut when I hear a cough—coming from inside Violet's closet.

What in the world?

Josiah tumbles out of the closet, falling to the floor. "Oh, hey, guys. Athena, what are you doing here?"

"I should be asking you that question. No, better yet, *why* were you hiding in the closet?"

Violet and Josiah stare at each other, no one saying a word.

"Stop communicating with your eyes. I'm starting to feel left out. Talk with words like normal people. It's not like you guys have anything to hide," I say, now really curious as to what is going on here.

Wait a second—

"*Do* you have something to hide?"

Violet's guilty face is all I need to see to know that she is definitely hiding something from me. "Okay, spill it."

Violet acts like she has no idea what I'm talking about. "Spill what?"

I'm not falling for it this time, though. "You're I-have-a-secret vibe is literally visible from the moon."

"Secret?" Violet laughs nervously. "Who says anything about a secret?"

"V—"

"Promise me you won't laugh."

Smiling, I shake my head. "I will make no such promises."

Josiah grabs Violet's hand, grinning. "We're dating."

"You're what—?" I can't stop the smirk that spreads on my face.

They are what?

"Wait, so what you're saying is... you and Josiah are dating *each other*?"

Violet nods. "Remember in elementary school when those reckless kids pushed you down the flight of stairs, V? You chipped your front tooth, and J"—I point right at Josiah—"made fun of you for weeks on end, even when he *knew* you were self-conscious about it?"

"Yeah." Violet laughs. "I remember."

"Okay, in *my* defense, I wasn't trying to hurt your feelings. I was just joking around," Josiah says, feeling the need to defend his honor.

"And that time you had a black eye, and J went around telling everyone you were experimenting with makeup, trying and failing for the *smoky eye* look. Is this the same Josiah we are talking about here?"

"Yep." Josiah winces, touching his eye. "I remember. That was the day you gave me a black eye to match."

"Well, you deserved it," Violet says, turning to punch him in the arm playfully.

"I know." Josiah kisses her hand.

"I think I'm going to be sick," I say, holding my stomach.

Violet grins, pulling Josiah and me into a group hug. "Oh, come here, you."

I'm happy as long as Violet is happy, and she looks thrilled.

They are an adorable couple.

"I am happy for you guys. Josiah, if you break her heart, you are so dead."

"Oh, I know. And trust me, I have no intention to." Josiah says with total confidence.

CHAPTER 38
Caiden:

I TRUDGE DOWN THE HARDWOOD stairs, my feet leading the way to the locked room at the end of the hallway. My palms are sweaty as I slowly turn the knob to my dad's old bedroom.

Massive pictures line the walls, a photo of Isabella and me as kids blowing rainbow-coloured bubbles in the backyard. Luna is running between us, completely mesmerized by the floating bubbles; she was only a pup back then.

I remember the day that Dad brought Luna home for us. Dad says that he always wanted to have a pet growing up, but they couldn't afford it. He wanted to make sure that we had everything that he couldn't have and more.

That was the kind of dad that he was.

On the nightstand by his iron bed sits a gold-framed photo of Mom, her eyes lit up with a bright smile; she looks happier here, more at ease, and carefree.

Dad made her so happy.

Next to the frame is his treasured recipe book. Though torn and bent with dog ears on the pages, Dad had cherished it. He was a phenomenal chef. Flipping through the pages, I notice that Dad had written inside some of the margins with notes such as, "No green onions for princess, add extra cilantro for my wife, and sautéed mushrooms for kiddo."

It wasn't until years later that I found out that Dad loved green onions. He was allergic to cilantro and mushrooms. Just the smell made him feel sick to his stomach. Yet, he made it. He catered to our likes and dislikes to give *us* what we wanted.

I turn the page, looking for the recipe that Dad and I always made together.

· · ᘛ · ·

In the kitchen, I dice up the tomatoes, spinach, and basil, mince the garlic, and then toss them into the cast-iron skillet, adding a little bit of avocado oil to sauté them in. Reaching under the cupboard, I look for a medium-sized pot to boil water for the pasta.

When the water comes to a boil, I add a pinch of salt. After the vermicelli noodles are finished cooking, I drain the water out of them and put the pot to the side while I work on the Rosé sauce. In a small pot, I add roasted tomatoes, spinach, garlic, basil, milk, and parmesan. While that is simmering, I stir-fry Cajun chicken and broccoli to pair with it.

Once the food is done, I put some on a plate, grab a fork from the silverware drawer, then head to the living room couch in front of the TV. Instead of eating, I just stare at the food, a lump forming in my throat. I can't bring myself to.

It's a painful reminder that Dad's not here anymore. And I hate it.

I miss him so much.

I wish Dad were here.

Flipping on the TV, I put on a movie, trying to distract myself from thinking about Dad. I find myself drawn to sad movies. Although I already know how they will end, I watch them anyway. Because happily ever after's are just made-up fairy tales, they *don't* exist.

Real life is tragic and miserable—we don't always get what we want in the end.

CHAPTER 39
Caiden:

"A PACKAGE CAME FOR you," Mom says, placing the brown box on the dresser in my room. "It's from Athena." She leaves, closing the door on her way out.

I bring the box to my bed, carefully untying the green ribbon. Inside the box, wrapped in polka dot tissue paper, is what looks like a charcoal-grey ceramic bowl with metallic gold streaks running through it.

I laugh to myself, thinking that the craftsmanship could use a *little* bit of work, but I admire her dedication.

Athena also included a handwritten letter. My curiosity is getting the better of me, and I'm eager to see what she has to say.

"Kintsugi is a Japanese art that takes broken pottery and delicately places it back together by sealing the cracks with gold lacquer. I found myself admiring the metaphor it represents.

It reminded me of you.

Maybe you feel you are broken inside. Maybe you're worried that you will disappoint me. Just like this pottery, life will never be perfect, but it can be beautiful. We must choose to see its beauty, not despite its cracks or imperfections, but because of it.

I get that you may not want to show me the side of you that's less than perfect, but don't you see?

I don't want perfect. Perfect is overrated.

All I want is you.

All that you are.

Exactly as you are.

I want you to know that I will wait for you for as long as it takes. Take your time. (but not too long)."

Her words bring warmth to my heart.

Flipping the paper to the other side, I see that there is another note there.

"P.S. Please pay no attention to the poor craftsmanship of the pottery. I'm an amateur at best. Violet gave up on helping me, saying I'd need a miracle to improve. I'm hoping with your help we can take another crack at this."

And just like that, I found myself unable to hold back anymore.

CHAPTER 40

Athena:

I'M IN THE LIVING ROOM trying any and everything to distract myself.

I've watched High School Musical one, two, and three. By now, I have re-watched it so many times that I have Gabriella and Troy's lines down pat and memorized every single duet. Even Sharpay and Ryan's.

Stuffing my face with a fist full of popcorn, I chomp down while yelling at the TV screen. "Come on, Sharpay, you *know* Troy never liked you. Stop it. You're embarrassing yourself." I shake my head. "Meanwhile, you ignore the guy that's *head over heels* for you. Poor Zeke! You deserve better, Zeke." My phone buzzes on the couch.

I lunge for it, hoping that it will be Caiden. I haven't heard from him in three days, 19 hours, and about 32 minutes. But, like, who's counting?

Not me, that's who.

I'm about to check to see who messaged me when Alex sits on my phone.

"Get up," I demand.

"Nope, don't feel like it," Alex says. He is being stubborn as usual.

"Seriously?" I sigh, annoyed. "Stop acting like a child and hand it over," I say while pulling his legs in a failed attempt to knock him off the couch so I can get my phone back.

"I'm doing you a favour." Alex doesn't even budge. "You will thank me later."

"Oh, please, I don't need your help. Thank you very much."

Alex laughs. "Oh really? How many times have you texted him?"

"Well..." Slipping the phone from under him, Alex unlocks my phone before I can stop him. "How do you know my password?"

"*Everyone* knows your password," Alex says, scrolling through the text messages on my phone.

"You are so uncool." He shakes his head disapprovingly. "I can't believe I'm related to you."

"I would ignore you too." Alex grimaces as he continues reading. "Have you ever heard of playing hard to get?"

I never understood the point in playing hard to get. All that does is waste precious time.

"Why would I do that?"

"Of course, you'd say something like that." Alex gives me back my phone, then collapses onto the couch beside me, flipping through the channels.

"He's probably going to break up with you," he says baldly.

I blinked, thinking that was *not* what I wanted to hear. But then again, Alex is just being Alex. He's never been one to sugarcoat things.

"What?" Alex asks, wondering what he said that was so wrong. "Was I *not* supposed to tell you the truth?"

I mean, it's not like Caiden would... could he be having second thoughts?

Does he want to break up with me?

I really hope that isn't the case... I really, really, *really* don't want things to end between us.

It would be too heartbreaking.

I look down at my phone. It turns out the text message *wasn't* from Caiden. It was from Ashley; I had asked her if we could meet up later.

Ashley: Sure, I'd love to. Should we meet up at the same place?

Ashley and I discovered this small little coffee place not too long ago. It is perfect because it is relatively unknown, which means it isn't busy and crowded like the other coffee shops around here. It's nice and quiet.

I type back; Sounds great to me. I'll meet you there.

. . ⤷ . .

The door chimes as I open it. Ashley is sitting at the far side of the room next to a big window. Pulling out the wooden bar stool across from her, I take a seat, smiling when I see that she's already ordered for me.

"You spoil me too much," I say, holding the warm mug of Cinnamon Apple Streusel tea in my hands. "Thank you."

"Anytime," Ashley says, taking a sip from her Crème Brule.

I smile, taking a bite of the double chocolate brownie Ashley got for us to share.

Caiden loves brownies.

I remember when Isabella and I made some, and he polished off half of the pan, leaving back just a few pieces for the rest of us. I scolded him for being so greedy, so he made up for it by bringing us Turtle's ice cream.

Turtle's ice cream, with brownies, was the *best* thing I never knew I needed.

I miss him so much.

"So, how are you?" Ashley asks gently.

Like mother, like son, they both have a way of doing that—a way of making me want to tell them how I really feel. "I'm okay, I guess. How is Caiden doing?" I stir my tea to mix the tea dust settling at the bottom of the cup.

Ashley slowly nods, her hands lingering on the gold chain around her neck. She notices me staring at it. "My husband... Caiden's father passed away."

"I'm so sorry." I wish I knew the right words to say, but all I can think of is how terrible that must have been for them.

Ashley gives me a weak smile. "Ever since Caiden's father died, he... he had no choice but to grow up." Ashley shakes her head, her eyes sad. "He became an adult too quickly; Caiden didn't get to... be just a kid."

Ashley says that Caiden busied himself taking care of them, and she was grateful for the help because, at the time, Ashley needed all the support she could get. When her husband died, she had no idea what to do without him.

Ashley didn't think she would *ever* have to do this on her own—raise her family alone.

"I was grateful for the help, but I knew... it wasn't right. Caiden shouldn't have felt like he *had* to."

I put a hand over Ashley's, trying to comfort her. "I was supposed to be the adult." Ashley shakes her head, her face serious.

"You did the best you could," I say softly, hoping to get through to her.

"But I should have done better."

I really had no idea of the immense sadness Ashley, Caiden, and Isabella had to live with.

My heart feels heavy in my chest. I'm worried about him. I want to reach out to Caiden and make sure he is okay.

But I can't.

I need to wait until he reaches out to me.

CHAPTER 41

Athena:

I LIE SPRAWLED OUT on my bed, anxiously staring at the phone in my hands.

I keep refreshing the page, hoping that maybe when I look back at it, I'll see that Caiden actually *did* reply, and I was the one that missed it.

Nope, nothing.

I toss my phone to the end of the bed and rolling to the other side, I pick up the book on my nightstand, deciding to read instead.

Unable to focus, I keep re-reading the same sentence over and over.

I know.

I know I promised to give him space, I tell myself as I pick up my phone from the edge of the bed, my fingers moving at lightning speed to send him another text.

Seven read messages and no reply.

Did my letter get lost in the mail?
I really hope not. Text me when you get it.
Are you okay?
If you are, I'm going to be really upset that you're ignoring me.
I lied. I have no patience, as you can probably already tell.
Call me?
Please.

Alex is right. I *am* a pathetic loser.

Maybe even worse, because I should feel some sense of shame for the way that I am acting, but I don't.

All I can think about is how much I miss him.

I wonder if—

The doorbell rings, breaking me out of my train of thought.

Could it be...

I catapult myself out of bed, running down the stairs to the door. I can barely contain my excitement when I open the door and see that it's Caiden.

Caiden is here, standing right in front of me, and I couldn't be happier.

"Hi," I say at the same time that Caiden asks, "Why?"

Caiden's sad face makes my smile fade away. "Why—why would you want to be with me?" he asks with his head bent; he cannot meet my eyes.

I try to take Caiden's hand, but he stuffs it into his pocket instead. "I have..." his voice comes out as a whisper. "Nothing to offer you."

I wish Caiden could be as kind to himself as he is to everyone else.

The fact that he doesn't see how *wonderful* he is breaks my heart into a million pieces.

"I don't want anything from you!" My voice shaking, I plead with Caiden, trying to get him to see himself from my point of view.

"You make me *so* happy." I smile through the tears shining in my eyes. "I thank God every day that I met you. I hate being apart from you; it hurts too much."

"I *really* missed you." Caiden stares at me, not saying anything, so I keep blabbering.

"I missed you so much that I couldn't think of anything else but you. Didn't you... miss me too?"

Caiden pulls me close, wrapping his arms tightly around me as he nestles his face into my hair. "All I ever do is miss you."

He pulls back, a broad smile appearing on his face.

I smile at him. "What?"

"I really, really, really missed you," he says in between showering my face with kisses.

I giggle, my heart feeling warm and full.

He kissed me again, then touched my face, gently running his fingers over my cheek. "Thank you for waiting for me."

A warm, fuzzy feeling settles over me like I'm curling into a blanket by a fire.

· · ❧ · ·

In the kitchen, I make two steaming cups of hot cocoa. Opening the fridge door, I take out a bottle of whip cream too because what's hot chocolate without whip cream? Pushing the nozzle on the top, I let the foam fizzle out in thick creamy layers.

"Tell me when to stop," I call out to him.

Caiden rests his hand under his chin, looking at me from over the back of the couch. He doesn't say anything as I continue adding more whipped cream. It is starting to look a lot like Mount Everest.

"Okay, that looks good. Thank you," Caiden says finally, reaching for the cup.

"No, that looks like *diabetes* in a cup." I sit down on the couch beside him.

Caiden shrugs, not seeing the big deal. "You are going to get diabetes, and they will have to amputate your foot." I turn to face him. "Is that what you want?"

"I'm fine with it." Caiden smiles cheekily. "As long as you are going to be there to take care of me, it's all good."

"That's under the assumption that I would stick around for that long."

"I guess time will tell," Caiden says, putting his mug on the coffee table.

We sit in comfortable silence for a bit, just enjoying each other's company.

"When I was younger... I used to really love looking up at the stars." He says, plopping his head on my lap. "You know, learning about them and going on trips to see them."

This is the first time that I am hearing about this.

I gently comb my fingers through his hair. "Is that why you got the telescope?"

"Yeah..."

"So how come you don't use it anymore?"

"Remember when you asked about the nightmare I had?" Swallowing hard, he looks up to meet my eyes. "It—it was about my dad."

He grows quiet as he struggles to get the words out.

I really feel bad now for asking so many questions. I don't want him to feel pressured to tell me.

"It's okay if you're not ready. You don't have to—"

Caiden squeezes my hand to assure me it's okay.

"He, umm... he died... in a car accident nine years ago. I was—I was in the car with him."

A car accident...

That explains Caiden's car sickness.

I stupidly thought he had motion sickness, but that wasn't the case... It was so much *more* than that.

He was *traumatized*.

I think back to what Ashley said earlier today at the coffee shop about Caiden wanting to protect them. It must have been so hard for him to be strong for so long.

I listen as Caiden's voice fills the room.

He tells me about the trip they had planned that day to see the Lunar Eclipse, of how he felt like he had pressured his dad to go—to keep his promise.

"The car that you saw in the garage... It's my dad's car. They wanted to trash it, but it's the only... It's all I have left. Every day I—I worked on it," Caiden says, the pain in his voice shattering my heart to pieces.

Tears well up in his eyes as he continues, "I promised that I wouldn't live that way again," he chokes out, wiping his eyes with the back of his hand. "The car was to... remind me of the consequences of being... of being selfish."

It must have been tremendously difficult for Caiden to open up and tell me about his dad, and I am so grateful that he did.

"I don't think you pushed him into doing what he didn't want to do." I stare at him, my cheeks wet with tears. "You *both* loved watching the stars. You just wanted to be with him because you love him, and there's no doubt in my mind that he loved you, too."

CHAPTER 42

Athena:

"YOU KNOW WHAT MY TEACHER says to us today at school?" Sky is perched at the edge of her seat at the kitchen table, obviously *dying* for someone to ask her about it.

But that's the thing; no one *wants* to because, well, Sky is such a teacher's pet.

She always goes on and on for ages, saying things like, 'My teacher said this' and 'My teacher said that.' We are all sick and tired of hearing about it.

Alex mimics Sky, trying to annoy her. "Shut up," Sky says, glaring at him.

Clearly oblivious to the fact that *no one* wants her to continue, Sky tells us what her teacher told her in class. "Prideful people are the loneliest because no one wants to befriend them."

A beat of silence passes.

Wow, for once, Sky's teacher said something remotely interesting. I'm pleasantly surprised.

"I don't have any friends," Rain says quietly.

"Well, if the shoe fits," Alex says, making us all laugh, except for Rain, of course.

"I don't know why *you're* laughing, Alex; you don't have any friends either," Rain fires back.

"But that's the fundamental difference between you and me." Alex points to Rain. "You care." He points back at himself. "And I *don't*."

He's got a valid point.

"Spell fundamental," Rain says.

"F. U. N. D—"

"Guys, enough," Mom interjects. "Alex, go chop up some wood for the bonfire. Collin, that barbeque isn't going to clean itself."

Collin kisses Mom on the cheek. "On it boss."

"Gross, get a room." Rain squirms, disgusted.

• • ⌗ • •

Half an hour later, the doorbell rings. "I'll get it!" Alex comes bounding down the stairs. He straightens his purple button-down shirt and takes a deep breath.

He opens the door, and a huge smile lights up his face. "Hi Jo-Anna," he says.

"Jo-Anna?" I whisper to Rain and Sky, who are just as shell-shocked as I am.

In walks a short, petite girl with beautiful curly hair. "Hello, it's so nice to meet all of you," Joanna says, smiling at us.

Mom wipes her hands on the dishcloth. "Hello, Jo-Anna. I'm Nicola, Alex's Mom."

"No way. You look like you could be Alex's older sister."

Mom blushes at the compliment.

"Well, thank you."

Jo-Anna gives Mom a bouquet of flowers. "These are lovely. I'll go put them in some water." Flattery can get you everywhere with Mom.

Jo-Anna shrugs off her coat. Alex takes it from her, like the perfect gentleman—shocking. "Here, I'll take that."

"She's too good for you," Sky pipes up.

"What?" Alex asks, so Sky feels the need to spell it out to him. "Jo-Anna. She's clearly out of your league." Sky gestures towards Alex. "I mean, look at you." Jo-Anna giggles.

"I really *like* her." Sky puts her hand out, and Jo-Anna shakes it. "Hi, I'm Sky. We are going to be the best of friends."

"I like the sound of that," Jo-Anna says.

. . ❧ . .

Caiden is the next to arrive. The second he sees Jo-Anna, he makes a beeline toward Alex, pulling him aside to the kitchen.

As an excuse to eavesdrop on their conversation, I ask Jo-Anna if she would like something to drink.

You know, being a good host and all.

"Yes, please," Jo-Anna says.

In the kitchen, I slowly open the fridge door to pour out some orange juice for Jo-Anna while also trying to listen in on the conversation between Caiden and Alex.

"Hey, is this the girl you were telling me about?" Caiden asks, grinning at Alex.

Since when were these two so chummy?

Alex nods, a sheepish smile on his face. "Yeah."

"No way, man. I'm so happy for you. Did you ask her out yet?"

"Obviously." Alex is smiling even more now. He looks happy.

Still, it's weird.

Alex has never brought a girl home before.

"Stop that," I say, stepping closer to the two of them, Jo-Anna's juice in my hands.

"Stop what?" Alex asks, directing his attention to me.

"Wipe that happy look off your face. It makes me sick." Caiden gives me a look that says he wants me to be nice.

I ignore it.

. . ❧ . .

I give Alex a stern warning as he and Jo-Anna head out the door to pick up more hotdogs and burgers for the barbeque.

"Alex Ashley Adams, you better be on your best behavior tonight or—"

Jo-Anna, who I thought was in the kitchen putting her glass away, asks, "Ashley?"

"Oops. I didn't *mean* for Jo-Anna to hear us. That was an accident, I promise. Oh well, cat's already out of the bag." I shrug innocently.

Alex closes his eyes, fuming; he *hates* his middle name.

My phone beeps.

A text message from Alex. Why would he text me when I'm standing right here?

Alex: YOU ARE SO DEAD.

Okay, so threatening me was totally unnecessary. It's not like I did it on purpose.

Then an evil thought enters my mind.

"Hey Jo-Anna, want to see the text that Alex just sent me?" Alex knocks the phone out of my hand onto the floor.

He's lucky it fell on the carpet.

Jo-Anna looks at him, an eyebrow raised. "Oh, you know... it was nothing." Alex chuckles, but it's forced. "Just the usual innocent sibling banter."

. . ✿ . .

Outside in the backyard, everyone else is here. Jake, Damon, Mel, Nessa, Violet, and Josiah. There's only one little teensy-weensy problem.

Other than Violet and Josiah, no one else knows yet that Caiden and I are dating...

I mean, it shouldn't be that big of a deal, but I know for sure that I will get teased relentlessly for this. I haven't seen them for a few months, and the first time I see them after so long... it will be interesting, there's no doubt about that.

Caiden, on the other hand, is full of bouncy smiles, ready to introduce me as his girlfriend, but I can't say I share his enthusiasm.

He pulls me into the backyard, holding my hand, and I feel anything but ready. Tightening the drawstring on my pink hoodie, I try to cover my face the best I can, letting my hair fall in front of me.

Ugh, this is so embarrassing.

"What are you *doing*?" Caiden tries to move the hair from in front of my face, and I slap his hand away. Through the slow-burning flame and smoke coming from the fire, I can feel everyone looking at me, which is only making me feel even more hot and stuffy.

Maybe I should go back inside.

And hide.

"We know it's you, Athena, so you can stop hiding now," Jake says, and everyone cracks up laughing. Reluctantly I pull down my hoodie. "Heyyy, guys."

Mel whistles while the others whoop and cheer us on.

"Oh, come on, A, we all knew you would end up together. You were the only one who didn't know," Nessa says, smiling.

Damon boasts that he takes all the credit for getting us together since it was him and Jake that kicked Caiden off his butt and got him to finally ask me out.

Jake runs over to hug me. "I missed you so much. I haven't seen you in forever." "Aw, I missed you too." I hug him back, and Jake nestles his face into my hair. Caiden peels Jake off of me. "Okay, that's enough."

It's so cute when he is jealous.

· · ⚘ · ·

Later, Jake asks if we want to play a round of basketball while we wait for the food to be ready. Caiden and I look at each other and start cracking up, both of us remembering the screen door incident.

"What's so funny?" Jake asks, wondering what we are laughing about.

I can barely even get a word out; tears are falling from my eyes. "It's... the..."

"That's... a... horrible... idea..." Caiden says, laughing even harder.

Every time Caiden and I look at each other it sends us into fits of manic laughter.

After we finally compose ourselves, we fill everyone in on what happened.

"We should totally re-enact that," Mel says.

I don't think so.

"Maybe we shouldn't do that. That was enough embarrassment to last a lifetime," I say, laughing.

. . ᴄ∽ᴀ . .

Collin fires up the barbeque, and smoke fills the air as he makes us grilled pineapple, bell peppers, and zucchini kabobs. Along with beef brisket, jerk chicken, burgers, and hot dogs.

We dig in, gobbling up everything on our plates.

"This is so good." I rub my stomach, feeling nice and full.

"Save room for dessert," Nessa says, pulling out the cinnamon roll waffles she brought.

"Oh, there is *always* room for dessert," I say, my mouth already watering, thinking about biting into them.

Alex heads inside to grab dessert plates for everyone.

"Hey, now is your chance," Caiden says, nudging me to go after him.

I told Caiden about the fight Alex and I had and how I planned to talk to Alex about it but haven't gotten around to it yet. I mean, what's the rush?

After all, we live in the same house together. There is plenty of time.

My eyes tell him I don't want to. "Come on," Caiden says, "you're going to forgive him eventually. Why not just do it now?"

"Ugh, do I have to?" Caiden gives me a look that tells me I don't have to, but he wants me to do it, anyway.

I groan, letting out a breath. "Fine."

. . ᴄ∽ᴀ . .

I slide open the patio door into the kitchen, where Alex has his hands full of paper plates. "Okay, fine. I admit I can be a *teensy* bit... dramatic... and maybe a bit irrational sometimes."

Alex raises an eyebrow, resting the plates on the counter. "Okay, fine, most of the time. But that's still no excuse for you not to be honest with me. You should have just told me the truth."

"You're right," Alex admits.

"Wait, what was that?" I ask in surprise.

"What?"

No *way* did I hear him correctly.

Alex just says that I was right.

"Want to say that again, just a *little* louder?"

Alex reluctantly repeats himself. "You were... right."

"One more time for the camera, please." I whip out my phone to record it.

Alex shakes his head, covering his face so I can't record him. "No flash photography."

I laugh at him while trying to move his hands away. He grabs onto my arms, stopping me. "So, are we cool?"

I laugh. Of course, we are. "Like the other side of the pillow."

"Great, because now would be a great time to mention that I may have broken your charger." "My what?" I ask, narrowing my eyes at him.

"Remember what we talked about?" Alex backs away slowly with his hands in front of him. "You promised not to be so overly dramatic."

"Oh, did I? I don't recall," I say as I slowly start walking towards him.

Alex laughs, thinking I'm joking.

I'm not.

"You've got ten seconds." My tone is now serious. "Ten, nine, eight..." I count, then chase him on seven seconds.

"You said ten!" Alex yells, flying out the patio door, knowing I won't chase him in front of an audience.

.. ❧ ..

Walking back to my seat beside Caiden, I pull out the red lawn chair. Caiden bites the inside of his cheek to keep from smiling. "I hate to say I told you so," he says.

Oh, please.

"Don't lie. You take pleasure from being right."

He nods, admitting it. "I do." I narrow my eyes at him.

"I'm sorry," Caiden says, but I know he does not mean it. He's clearly happy.

I cross my arms over my chest, turning around in my chair to face him. "How can you say sorry with a smile on your face? You obviously aren't sorry."

Caiden's face breaks out into a grin. "I'm sorry, I'm *not* sorry."

I shake my head, laughing at him.

CHAPTER 43

Athena:

I'M DRIVING HOME ON my way back from work when I decide to stop over at Caiden's house.

Isabella lets me in. I hear running water in the kitchen, so I go over to ask Ashley if she needs some help.

"Can I get you anything, Hun?"

An older lady, who I assume might be Isabella's grandmother, smiles at me as she wipes her hands on her apron.

I can see where Ashley gets her smile from. They have the same warm smile. "Oh, um, I'm okay. It's sweet of you to offer. You must be Isabella's grandmother."

"Yes, sweet pea, I am. Let me guess; you must be Athena."

"Yeah, how did you—"

"I've heard *so* much about you," she says with such sweetness in her voice.

"Good things, I hope." I smile awkwardly.

"Most definitely."

She pulls out a chair for me to take a seat as she brings a cup of tea. "You can call me Rosa."

"That's a beautiful name." I look to Luna's favourite chair. "I don't see Luna around today."

"Oh, she's with Ashley, keeping her company," Rosa says, sitting beside me and setting down a plate of Pistachio Biscotti. "I'm just here for a few days to watch Isabella while her Mom's at the hospital."

"Hospital?" My mouth goes dry.

"Yes. Oh, dear." Rosa puts a hand to her chest. "Did no one tell you?" I continue to look at her, my eyes wide with shock.

"Caiden gave us a bit of a scare on Friday night. So, we brought him over to the hospital last night." Before she can even finish telling me what happened, I'm already up and headed for the door.

"Thank you for the tea!" I call out as I close the door.

I can't believe him.

Why didn't he tell me?

· · ᜑᜒ · ·

On the drive over, I can't help but think about what kind of state I might see him in.

He doesn't normally let me see this side of him, but I don't care. I'm going anyway, and he's not going to stop me.

My heart is pounding as I walk through the hospital, looking for the right floor. I see the reception area on the right, so I walk right over and ask which room Caiden's staying in. I have an unsettling feeling about this.

"Caiden Alshaaer?" The lady at the front desk taps away on her keyboard, scrolling through the list of names.

"Yes."

"How do you know him? Are you a relative?" she asks. I know it's her job to ask, but I just hope she doesn't stop me from going to see him.

"His girlfriend."

Flipping a page on her clipboard, she tells me, "He's in room number 405."

"Thank you." I don't bother to wait for the elevator. Running up the stairs, taking two at a time, I'm huffing and puffing as my eyes scan the halls, looking for his room number.

Caiden:

"WHAT A JERK!" ATHENA yells as she storms into my hospital room.

"I see your hot temper hasn't changed," I say with a smirk.

"Why didn't you tell me you weren't feeling okay?" Athena says, taking in the IV stuck into my arm and the IV fluids hanging over me.

I didn't want her to worry about me. I figured it would be best if she didn't know.

It's not like it's the first time I've been to the hospital after an episode. They just need to pump me with some Alemtuzumab, and I'll be out of here in no time.

Athena looks at me with tear-stricken eyes. "Are you okay?"

"Well..." I flash her a smile. "My eyebrows don't hurt."

She cracks the tiniest smile, then frowns again.

"Seriously though, if you are in pain, I need you to tell me." Her voice is stern, commanding.

Hoping to lighten the mood, I continue, "Hey, remember that time we went to see that Shakespeare play at Rose Valley Theatre? It was supposed to be a super extravagant, classy night out. But *someone* couldn't stop laughing at the guy in the crazy red pants."

"Ugh. Must you remind me of that dreadful day?" She groans.

I laugh, clutching my stomach, although I know I shouldn't because the motion makes my head spin. "You laughed so hard you snorted pop out of your nose. It went flying!"

"You're never going to let me live that one down, are you?"

"I just can't get over how funny it was. The look on your face when the couple in front of us turned around disgusted was *priceless*. You looked like you wanted to evaporate and die."

Athena laughs, too. "He's lucky I didn't bring popcorn too; it would have been *all* over the then."

Then her face is back to being serious. "It's *okay* not to be okay... if you're in pain, you are *allowed* to cry." She wraps her arms around my neck. "Don't hold it all inside. Promise me that you'll tell me next time."

Her chocolate brown eyes meet mine, making my chest fill with warmth.

I pull her close, softly kiss her cheeks, and then, finally, her lips. "I promise."

CHAPTER 44

Caiden:

"HEY, SWEETIE," MOM says, wiping the tears with the back of her hand.

Mom blames the onions for making her cry.

My heart aches at the tears forming in her eyes as she sautés the onions on the stove.

My mom is... superhuman. Aside from Dad's funeral, I had never seen her shed a single tear. She stepped right back into the swing of things, making her focus remain on Isabella and me. Mom wanted to make sure we didn't feel like we were missing out on anything.

I remember the shiny new purple bike that Dad bought for Isabella. It was sitting on the porch, unridden. Isabella cried and cried that Dad promised to teach her how to ride her bike. Back then, we didn't know how to explain that Dad had died. At the tender age of four, Isabella didn't understand what death meant, and who could blame her? Even as adults, we cannot come to terms with death, so how could a child? Isabella really thought that Dad went on a trip but would eventually come back. Mom ended up being the one who taught Isabella how to ride a bike.

My mind keeps swirling back to the pained expression on her face when I came home early that day, and it's killing me.

"Stop," I hear myself say.

Stop acting like you're okay.

You're *not* okay; it's not okay.

Mom moves to the counter to dice up the remaining onion to add it to the pan on the stove.

"I'll do it," I say. Taking the knife from Mom's hands, I cut the onion in half and chop away.

As much as I would like to just tuck it away, I can't escape this agonizing pain that washes over me.

Mom stands beside me, but I refuse to make eye contact with her. The weight of unsaid words hangs in the silence.

Mom watches me intently as if she has something she wants to say, but it seems she thinks better of it because she sighs and walks away.

"It's my fault." The sound of my quivering voice breaks the silence.

"What?" Mom asks as she turns around to look at me.

Eyes downcast, I force myself to say the words out loud. "The car accident. It's—" My voice trembles as I struggle to get the words out. "It's my fault."

Mom stares at me in disbelief, a mix of horror and agony crosses her face. "No, baby, no. Why... why would you say that?" Tears brim her eyes.

"He just... just wanted... to make me happy. But stupid me didn't see that he was so tired. I shouldn't have pushed him to go! If I hadn't... he would still be alive!" I yell in frustration, hating myself for what I did, for tearing our family apart.

Dropping the knife, I cover my face with my hands and try to hold back the tears forming in my eyes.

Walking over, Mom wraps her arms around me. "I'm sorry." She cries into my arms. "I'm so... so sorry, baby. I've been incredibly selfish and a horrible mother. I was so caught up in my own pain I failed to see yours. Of course not! It's not your fault. It was *never* your fault."

Mom rubs my back, and, unable to hold back anymore, my face crumples as I break down and cry.

I feel like I've been holding my breath all this time. I start to feel at ease as I finally let it go.

"Your dad would be so incredibly proud of you," Mom says, looking at me with tear-stricken eyes.

"He would?" I ask, finding it hard to believe. I've been so scared my whole life that I could never live up to... I just wished that I could make my father proud.

To make him as happy as he made me.

"Of course, and so am I. You are, in the *best* way possible, your father's son."

All I've ever wanted was to be even *half* the man that Dad was. He was as good as they get. So, to know that my dad would be *proud* of me... Words can't even begin to describe how happy and relieved that makes me feel.

I want to soak up this feeling and make it last forever.

CHAPTER 45

Athena:

I AM PACING BACK AND forth, my palms drenched with sweat as I anxiously wait on the front porch of our house.

I've made a decision.

And I'm going to stick with it. Once this is done, there is *no* going back.

I nervously bite my lower lip as I continue to refresh the screen on my phone, waiting for the time to say 6:30 p.m.

6:25.

Okay, he will be here in five minutes.

I take a sharp breath, trying to calm my nerves. I can do this.

Athena, you can do this.

He arrives at six-thirty on the dot, right on time, slowly making his way out of the car, walking up the stone patio steps to where I stand.

He keeps a distance of about three feet between us. I study the look on Dad's face, the crease in his brows.

He looks just as uneasy about this as I am.

I'm ready to let it go, to move forward. I asked Dad to meet with me today so we could end this once and for all.

"Hi," Dad says, with a warm smile on his face.

The look in his eyes makes it even harder for me to compose myself. "I can't—I can't do this anymore."

"I'm just... so *tired,* okay?" My throat starts to close up, but I'm a big girl now, and big girls don't cry. My body betrays me, though, as my voice comes out as only a whisper. "Tired of hating you."

Everyone was right all along. Holding on to hurt feelings was only hurting me.

I slowly came to the conclusion that harboring anger and resentment is not the way to live.

That is not how I *want* to live.

Not anymore.

As he steps toward me ever so cautiously, I can see that Dad's eyes are red and puffy. The wrinkles beside his eyes tell me he's getting old. "Baby girl, I'm sorry. I'm sorry I hurt you. I never—never should have let you down. I... don't deserve your forgiveness, but if you would let me, I will spend the rest of my life making it up to you."

Dad's hands are on my arms now, his eyes pleading with me to forgive him.

To let him back in.

To trust him.

He must see how torn up I feel inside because I can see the tears shining in his eyes. Dad closes the space between us, wrapping his arms around me. "I do... I forgive you," I choke out, hot salty tears springing from my eyes.

It was at that moment that I realized how much I missed it. A place I thought I had forgotten about is suddenly alive and overflowing with emotions I didn't even know I had as I completely unravel in my father's warm embrace.

THE END.

If you enjoyed this book, please consider leaving a review on Amazon[1] **or** Goodreads[2] **and recommend it to a friend. >**

I would be so, so grateful for any words you might be willing to leave!

If you want to stay in the know about the All That You Are *sequel* join my newsletter[3] or follow me on Instagram[4]!

---

1.   https://mybook.to/Allthatyouare

2.   https://www.goodreads.com/book/show/59831284-all-that-you-are

3.   https://docs.google.com/forms/d/e/1FAIpQLSdiYfhMnaT9whhz0jDH9yLHJujZK7euoh8wuWmTlypo-jz6QkQ/viewform

4.   https://www.instagram.com/eliciaroper/

To hear the *inspiration* behind All That You Are, continue reading to see the Author's Note & Getting Help Resources.

Author's Note

I DEBATED FOR A WHILE whether or not I wanted to include this Author's Note because *All That You Are* is not a story about mental health. However, it is a fiction story that conveys the *truth* about my battle with mental health.

I started writing *All That You Are* at a time in my life where, like Caiden, I struggled to forgive myself and to allow myself to be happy. Caiden's character came so naturally to me because we both view ourselves as broken; too far gone to be fixed.

Writing became therapeutic for me.

It allowed me to see my innermost thoughts and feelings and creatively weave them into a story—a story where Caiden and I can forgive ourselves and choose to be happy. This novel shed light on my internal struggle with my mental health. It made me brave enough to get the help I desperately needed.

Through Caiden and Athena's characters, I realized how much I want to be *truly* happy.

That's why the theme of *All That You Are* is forgiveness—for Caiden to forgive *himself* and for Athena to forgive her *dad*. Forgiveness leads to true happiness.

I hope this book heals you in the many ways it has comforted and healed me.

Dealing with mental health can be lonely and scary, and unfortunately, there is still so much stigma around mental health, which makes getting help even more difficult.

That's why I would like you to know that you have *nothing* to be ashamed of.

Accepting help and treatment doesn't make you weak; it makes you *strong* and *brave*. I strongly encourage you to reach out to someone you trust: a parent, a friend, a counselor, or a therapist. Visit the resources I've listed for you below. There are people out there waiting to be on your side. To receive help, you must take the first step by *talking* to someone. It may feel scary and intimidating, especially if you've never done it before. But prioritizing your health is of utmost value.

You are important, and you *deserve* to feel loved and to be *happy*.

You are not alone.

Getting Help

MENTAL HEALTH RESOURCES - Canada
Wellness together Canada
Wellness Together Canada | Home[1]
1-866-585-0445

Wellness Together Canada was created in response to an unprecedented rise in mental health and substance use concerns due to the COVID-19 pandemic, with funding from the Government of Canada. As a country, we are facing challenges at a scale we've never seen before, from social isolation and financial insecurity to substance use concerns and racial inequality.

We may be physically apart, but we're all in this together at the end of the day. We believe that wellness is a journey, not a destination—and every day, we can each take a step toward our well-being. Wellness Together Canada is here to support you on that journey.

Wellness Together Canada also offers Text SMS Therapy
Text: **741741**
Mental Health COAST hotline:
Crisis Outreach and Support Team (COAST) (stjoes.ca)[2]
24-hour COAST Crisis Line
905-972-8338

COAST (Crisis Outreach and Support Team) provides services to people experiencing a crisis related to mental health and addictions. COAST is a unique partnership between mental health professionals

---

1. https://wellnesstogether.ca/en-CA

2. https://www.stjoes.ca/health-services/mental-health-addiction-services/mental-health-services/coast

from St. Joseph's Healthcare Hamilton and specially trained police officers from the Hamilton Police Service.

COAST answers crisis telephone calls 24 hours a day, seven days a week. All phone calls are answered or returned within 15 minutes. COAST can also see people in the community between 8 a.m. and 1 a.m. daily to provide mobile mental health assessments and in-person support.

Canada Suicide Prevention Service Hotline

Canada Suicide Prevention Service | Crisis Services Canada[3]

1-833-456-4566

If you need support, call us now at our toll-free number **1.833.456.4566.** We are available 24x7x365. You will not incur long-distance charges for your call.

We offer support to anyone concerned about suicide. Whether you are suffering from a loss, worried about someone who may have suicidal thoughts, or having suicidal thoughts yourself, our highly trained responders are there to provide support. Talking about suicide can open the door for effective dialogue about the intense emotional pain and enable someone to see what steps need to be taken to ensure safety, whether it's your own or the safety of someone you care about. Connecting with someone about your suicidal thoughts is life-saving.

Connect through Text 4pm-12am

Text: **45645**

Reaching out can be scary, but taking that step—by text or phone—can help you feel less alone when you need it the most.

For some people in distress, reaching out and talking on the phone can be intimidating, especially for anyone who uses text as their usual form of communication.

Many people find it easier to express emotion by typing than by talking out loud.

---

3. https://www.crisisservicescanada.ca/en/

The responders who answer your texts are there to support you in the struggles you are facing.

They can help you explore ways to create safety when things are feeling out of control.

Mental Health Resources – United States

• • ⌘ • •

National Suicide Prevention Lifeline

The National Suicide Prevention Lifeline is a national network of more than 150 local crisis centers. It offers free and confidential emotional support around the clock to those experiencing a suicidal crisis.

Contact information:

800-273-8255 (24/7)

Online chat: https://suicidepreventionlifeline.org/chat/ (24/7)

https://suicidepreventionlifeline.org/

Crisis Text Line

The Crisis Text Line is a free text messaging resource offering 24/7 support to anyone in crisis. Since August 2013, more than 79 million text messages have been exchanged.

The Veterans Crisis Line

The Veterans Crisis Line is a free, confidential resource staffed by qualified responders from the Department of Veterans Affairs. Anyone can call, chat, or text — even those not registered or enrolled with the VA.

Contact information:

800-273-8255 and press 1 (24/7)

Text **838255** (24/7)

Online chat: www.veteranscrisisline.net/get-help/chat[4] (24/7)

Support for those who are deaf or hard of hearing: 800-799-4889

www.veteranscrisisline.net[5]

---

4.   http://www.veteranscrisisline.net/get-help/chat

SAMHSA's National Helpline (Substance Abuse)

The Substance Abuse and Mental Health Services Administration's (SAMHSA) national helpline offers confidential treatment referrals in both English and Spanish to people struggling with mental health conditions, substance use disorders, or both. In the first quarter of 2018, the helpline received more than 68,000 calls every month.

Contact information:

800-662-HELP (4357) (24/7)

TTY: 800-487-4889 (24/7)

www.samhsa.gov/find-help/national-helpline[6]

• • ༄ • •

Mental Health Resources – UK

SANEline. If you're experiencing a mental health problem or supporting someone else, you can call SANEline on **0300 304 7000** (4.30pm–10.30pm every day).

• • ༄ • •

National Suicide Prevention Helpline UK. Offers a supportive listening service to anyone with thoughts of suicide. You can call the National Suicide Prevention Helpline UK on **0800 689 5652** (6pm–3:30am every day).

• • ༄ • •

Campaign Against Living Miserably (CALM). You can call the CALM on **0800 58 58 58** (5pm–midnight every day) if you are struggling and need to talk. Or if you prefer not to speak on the phone, you could try the CALM webchat service.

• • ༄ • •

---

5.   http://www.veteranscrisisline.net/

6.   http://www.samhsa.gov/find-help/national-helpline

Shout. If you would prefer not to talk but want some mental health support, you could text SHOUT to **85258**. Shout offers a confidential 24/7 text service providing support if you are in crisis and need immediate help.

. . ⚘ . .

The Mix. If you're under 25, you can call The Mix on **0808 808 4994** (3pm–midnight every day), request support by email using this form on The Mix website or use their crisis text messenger service.

. . ⚘ . .

Papyrus HOPELINEUK. If you're under 35 and struggling with suicidal feelings, or concerned about a young person who might be struggling, you can call Papyrus HOPELINEUK on **0800 068 4141** (weekdays 10am-10pm, weekends 2pm-10pm and bank holidays 2pm–10pm), email pat@papyrus-uk.org or text 07786 209 697.

. . ⚘ . .

C.A.L.L. If you live in Wales, you can call the Community Advice and Listening Line (C.A.L.L.) on **0800 132 737** (open 24/7) or you can text 'help' followed by a question to **81066**.

. . ⚘ . .

Mind.org.uk: Advice and support to anyone experiencing a mental health problem. Their services include supported housing, crisis helplines, drop-in centers, employment and training programs and counselling. Their lines are open 9 a.m. to 6 p.m., Monday to Friday (excluding bank holidays) on **0300 123 3393 or by text message on 86463**.

Getconnected.org.uk: Get Connected is a free, confidential telephone and email helpline which finds young people the best help whatever the problem may be. They provide free connections to local and national services and can text you information, too. Call any day of the week from 1 p.m. to 11 p.m. on **0808 808 4994**

· · ⚬ · ·

Talktofrank.com: FRANK is an honest and open resource to find out anything you might want to know about drugs. For friendly, confidential, and judgement-free advice for anyone concerned about their own or someone else's drug or solvent use, call on **0800 77 66 00**. This is free if called from a landline, and it won't show up on your phone bill. They provide free translation services for non-English speakers. FRANK also has a live-chat service

About The Author

THANK YOU FOR reading All That You Are! I hope you loved it as much as I loved writing it! If you want to stay in the know about the All That You Are *sequel* join my newsletter[1], or follow me on Instagram[2]!

You can find me online at-

Instagram:@eliciaroper[3]

Tiktok:@authoreliciaroper[4]

Goodreads: All That You Are by Elicia Roper | Goodreads[5]

Website: @eliciaroper | Linktree[6]

Thank you, dear reader, you made my dream a reality. If you loved Athena and Caiden's story, please consider leaving a review on Amazon[7] or Goodreads![8]

Lots of love,

Elicia

1. https://docs.google.com/forms/d/e/1FAIpQLSdiYfhMnaT9whhz0jDH9yLHJujZK7euoh8wuWmTlypojz6QkQ/ viewform

2. https://www.instagram.com/eliciaroper/

3.   https://www.instagram.com/eliciaroper/

4.   https://www.tiktok.com/@authoreliciaroper

5.   https://www.goodreads.com/book/show/59831284-all-that-you-are

6.   https://linktr.ee/eliciaroper

7.   https://www.amazon.com/dp/B09MZMMLLS

8.   https://www.goodreads.com/book/show/59831284-all-that-you-are

Lightning Source UK Ltd.
Milton Keynes UK
UKHW020630230223
417504UK00011B/1360